A Candlelight Ecstasy Romance ®

"ALL THAT COUNTS IS WHAT YOU WANT RIGHT NOW," HE WHISPERED HUSKILY.

Her entire body throbbed achingly for his caresses, and with an agonized moan of defeat, she caught his hands in her own. He had won. She wrapped her arms around him as his masterful lips took the softness of hers again and again in long, dangerously deepening kisses that soon induced in her a boneless acquiescence. She wanted to go on touching him forever . . .

A CANDLELIGHT ECSTASY ROMANCE ®

DANGEROUS EMBRACE

Donna Kimel Vitek

A CANDLELIGHT ECSTASY ROMANCE ®

Published by
Dell Publishing Co., Inc.
1 Dag Hammarskjold Plaza
New York, New York 10017

Dell ® TM 681510, Dell Publishing Co., Inc.

Candlelight Ecstasy Romance®, 1,203,540, is a registered
trademark of Dell Publishing Co., Inc., New York, New
York.

ISBN: 0–440–12162–0

Printed in the United States of America
First printing—April 1983

To Our Readers:

We have been delighted with your enthusiastic response to Candlelight Ecstasy Romances®, and we thank you for the interest you have shown in this exciting series.

In the upcoming months we will continue to present the distinctive sensuous love stories you have come to expect only from Ecstasy. We look forward to bringing you many more books from your favorite authors and also the very finest work from new authors of contemporary romantic fiction.

As always, we are striving to present the unique absorbing love stories that you enjoy most—books that are more than ordinary romance.

Your suggestions and comments are always welcome. Please write to us at the address below.

Sincerely,

The Editors
Candlelight Romances
1 Dag Hammarskjold Plaza
New York, New York 10017

DANGEROUS EMBRACE

CHAPTER ONE

Kate Austin sat back in her swivel chair. Tucking a strand of thick chestnut hair back behind one ear, she gazed thoughtfully at the worried woman across the desk from her. "Actually, I might have an answer to your problem, Mary," she said at last, her soft pleasant voice conveying genuine understanding. "It might sound a bit drastic to you at first, but I think it would be the best solution all the way around. I hope you'll think so."

"Oh, I'm sure I will. Really, Miss Austin, I'm desperate. I just have to have the next three or four weeks off to be with Jimmy. I can't begin to tell you how awful it's been the past ten days," Mary Weaver murmured thickly, lips atremble. "Meningitis is such a horrible thing and with Jimmy barely a year old . . . Well, now that he's out of danger, and we'll be able to take him home pretty soon, I just feel like I have to stay out with him for a while. Right now he really needs his mama with him."

"I agree. You should stay with him until he's completely well. All of this must have been very frightening to him. And you," Kate said, green eyes darkening with compassion. "But instead of simply telling you your job will be waiting for you if you take off three or four weeks, I have another idea. We're going to have to lay some people off temporarily anyway, so why shouldn't you be one of them?"

"Laid off?" Mary exclaimed, a distinct quaver in her voice. "But, Miss Austin, I didn't mean I wanted to give up my job here. I thought you knew I only wanted a few weeks off. Please . . ."

Tiny dimples appeared on either side of Kate's mouth as she smiled and lifted a silencing hand. "Mary, you must know we wouldn't think of letting you go permanently. You've worked in this store nearly ten years, and we consider you one of our most valuable employees. No one knows the Miss Sophisticate department the way you do. So we certainly don't intend to let you give up your job here. The layoffs I mentioned are only *temporary*. I fully expect almost everyone to be rehired in a month or so. Normally, I'd never think of laying you off, but since you need a leave of absence anyway, this seems the logical solution. You'll have the time you need with your little boy, and one of the other employees here will be able to continue working."

"Well, that does make sense," Mary conceded, though a slight frown still marred her brow. "If you're sure I'll be rehired in—"

"I'm sure. Please don't worry."

"But the new management . . ."

"Before the Renaldo family sold the store to the Barron chain, they were guaranteed the entire staff here would be retained," Kate said, leaning forward to rest her arms on her desk as she smiled reassuringly at the older woman. "And besides, being laid off temporarily would be better for you. You'll be able to collect unemployment benefits without seeking new employment because you already have a job to come back to in a few weeks. That's North Carolina law, but if you were permanently laid off, you'd have to actively seek work to receive benefits."

"You mean I can count on a little money coming in the next three or four weeks?" Mary asked, tears of sheer relief filling her eyes. "Oh, Miss Austin, I can't tell you how much that will mean to my family. All these medical expenses . . . And this will help a little."

Kate nodded. "Good. If this arrangement keeps you from worrying as much, you'll have more time and energy to put into helping Jimmy recover completely."

As Mary rose to her feet, she looked years younger than she had when she had entered Kate's office earlier. "You've been so very kind," she said sincerely. "I'm glad I came to talk to you instead of seeing Mr. Meadows. I know he has a lot of responsibilities as personnel director, but he does seem kind of cold sometimes."

"I don't think he means to be. Joe just tends to get preoccupied," Kate explained, feeling compelled to defend the man she was romantically involved with, though she understood what Mary meant. Joe Meadows occasionally could be annoyingly straitlaced and intolerant, but basically he wasn't like that. Standing behind her desk, she nodded confidently. "I'm sure if you'd taken your problem to Joe, he'd have been very understanding."

"Maybe," Mary agreed rather reluctantly but smiled as she started toward the door. "I'm still glad I came to see you, though. I don't know how to thank you for all your help, Miss Austin."

"You might start by calling me Kate, the way you always used to when I was a clerk in your department. What's this Miss Austin business? Good heavens, you've known me six years, since I came here to work part-time."

"I know, but things changed. After you finished school and were promoted to assistant personnel manager, I just didn't think I should be so familiar." Mary grimaced almost comically. "You know, some people get kind of snooty when they move up in the world. I didn't think you had, but I couldn't be exactly sure."

"I won't take that as an insult," Kate teased, going round her desk to open the door for the older woman. "Now, run along to the hospital and see how Jimmy is this morning. And stop worrying about work. If there's anything I can do to help you, just call me."

After Mary expressed her appreciation one last time and rushed away, Kate left her office to walk past the reception desk to a bank of file cabinets. She removed Mary's file then six others, and when she pushed the last drawer shut, she breathed a sigh. Though Mary's temporary layoff had proved a godsend, Kate was fairly certain the other six employees she would have to speak to today wouldn't be thrilled to hear they were to be out of work for a month or so. Unemployment benefits simply didn't make up for weekly wages, so this was going to be a disappointing day for six people. Letting employees go, even temporarily, was the one part of her job that Kate absolutely loathed, but she supposed that this time it was truly a necessary evil. The store was experiencing a seasonal lull in sales, and with a representative of the new owners arriving today to monitor operations for a month or two, it wouldn't be wise to have salesclerks standing idly in their departments twiddling their thumbs.

To make certain she had chosen the employees who had been with Renaldo's the least amount of time, Kate began glancing through the files she held. As she turned away from the cabinets, she drew in a swift half-startled breath when she practically stumbled over the person standing directly behind her. Her eyes darted up from the lapels of a brown suit and darker brown tie to Joe Meadows's pleasantly attractive face, and she felt a nearly overwhelming desire to tell him to stop sneaking up on her that way. It was a desire she valiantly suppressed, though the smile she gave in response to his felt rather forced and weak as it pulled upward on her lips.

"Another day, another dollar," Joe said as usual, glancing quickly around the office before gliding his hands beneath Kate's forearms. Stepping even closer, he lowered his voice. "You look too pretty for me to resist kissing you, but I'd better do it now before the new owner's spy descends on us."

After looking around the office once more to make certain no one else was nearby, Joe brushed a haphazard and thoroughly uninspiring kiss across Kate's lips. He rushed away then, and feeling suddenly quite disgruntled, she watched him go. Joe's secretive, almost furtive kisses were beginning to get on her nerves, and she wasn't sure why. She certainly didn't want him to sweep her into his arms in a passionate clinch; she really preferred no displays of affection at the office, but at the same time she found Joe's sneaky kisses increasingly irritating. Though she couldn't see what real harm it would do for someone to witness an occasional peck on her cheek, Joe was horrified at the very possibility. And she thought it was rather priggish of him to insist on concealing the fact that they were now seeing each other socially. Nothing was wrong with their personal relationship since neither of them were married, and Joe's too cautious attitude rubbed Kate the wrong way.

"Everything rubs you the wrong way these days," she murmured, hugging the files against her breasts as she went to the window and stared out unseeingly at Raleigh's domed capitol building. Sighing heavily again, she wondered what on earth had happened to make her feel so out of sorts recently. Until about six weeks ago, she had been reasonably content, but now she was easily annoyed, and not only by Joe. Except when she could immerse herself in work, she felt every aspect of her life was smothering her with sheer, unabated tedium. She was almost constantly bored yet had no idea why, which added considerably to her sense of frustration. For a while, she had hoped she was simply suffering an acute case of spring fever but now it was June. Spring had come and gone, and she still felt as if the walls were closing in.

Shaking her head as if to reassemble her thoughts, Kate turned from the window and walked resolutely back into her office to proceed with the job at hand. By ten thirty, she had seen the six employees the store was letting go temporarily. After the last young salesclerk left, collective disappointment seemed to hang like a pall around Kate's desk, and to keep her mind off the unpleasant but necessary task she had just performed, she hastily immersed herself in the last monthly sales report.

It was nearly twenty minutes later when Molly, the personnel receptionist, excitement dancing over her pretty gamine face, knocked once on Kate's door before opening it to peek inside the office.

"Come out, Kate, hurry. *He's* here!" she announced dramatically. "Or at least he'll be here in just a minute. Jo Ann just called and said Mr. Tilford is showing him around, starting here first. So, come on. Jo talked like he's plenty good-looking."

Realizing *he* must be the new owner's representative, Kate nodded. "Be out in a moment," she said and smiled, as Molly quickly disappeared, apparently eager to catch her first sight of *him*. Unfortunately, she and her friend Jo Ann, the receptionist in the executive suite, considered any reasonably attractive man "plenty good-looking," so Kate was fairly certain this one wouldn't be a Robert Redford look-alike. Still, she wanted to make a good first impression. She ran a comb through gently curled hair that just grazed her shoulders, then smoothed her skirt as she stood. Though the neat rust-colored suit she wore covered but could not completely conceal the very adequate curves of her slender body, she knew she looked sufficiently efficient and businesslike.

Kate stepped out of her office at the same moment Mr. Tilford, the store manager, and Molly's Man of the Day were entering the reception area. Immediately, the low buzz of voices ceased. All eyes turned toward the doorway, but Kate couldn't see because Joe stood beside the reception desk right in her line of vision. Wry amusement touched her softly shaped lips as she noticed how everyone was standing at attention as if this were a lowly army barracks undergoing a surprise inspection by a five-star general. Her low-heeled pumps glided noiselessly across the carpet as she moved to Joe's side. Then her smile froze on her lips, and she stopped breathing for several long seconds after seeing the man who was with Mr. Tilford. For an instant the room actually seemed to spin. She blinked her eyes, but that didn't alter the too familiar lineation of the man's long lean powerful body nor the carved profile of his tanned face. It was Nathan—and Kate, nearly overwhelmed by the need to run away, was briefly panic-stricken.

Sheer will power prevented such cowardice, and Kate stood perfectly still, her dark troubled gaze sweeping over Nathan Cordell as he turned away while Mr. Tilford introduced him to someone on the opposite side of the room. A host of memories swirled through her brain, and only one lucid thought came out of them—Nathan looked exactly the same after six years. His thick dark hair still touched the top of his back collar in the same way, and somehow that tiny detail brought tears to her eyes. Kate fought them. Her jaw tensed as she dragged up from the very depth of her being all the self-control she could muster. Yet her eyes remained riveted on Nathan's broad back. He had been her first and only lover, and for a few idyllic weeks, when she was nineteen, she had adored him. Then, a month before her twentieth birthday, she had ended their relationship because she had realized his feelings for her were neither lasting nor serious, and she could no longer cope with the burden of guilt they shared. Together they had caused irreparable harm to other people, yet leaving Nathan had been an agonizing experience. It had taken more years than she liked to remember to recover completely from the pain of it. Now here he was, stirring up memories and feelings better left forgotten. And she didn't understand. *What was he doing here?* Nothing made sense.

Desperate for an explanation, she laid a hand on Joe's forearm, unaware that her nails pressed down hard as she whispered, "Why is he here? Nathan Cordell! The Renaldo stores were bought by the Barron chain, so why has he come? Do you know?"

A puzzled frown creased Joe's brow but he nodded. "The Cordells bought the Barron chain two or three months ago. Sort of a quiet, uneventful merger. But what's the matter with you? You look kind of funny."

Immediately, Kate arranged her face in more composed lines. "I . . . uh, nothing's the matter. I just wondered why he was here."

"How did you even know him? Oh, that's right; you worked in the Cordell's in Charlotte for a while, didn't you?" Joe nodded, quite satisfied with his own explanation. "You probably saw him then, but I don't suppose you actually knew him?"

"I knew him," Kate answered woodenly, still too much in shock to even attempt a lie. She only noticed Joe's questioning stare when it was suddenly averted because Mr. Tilford was quickly making introductions around the semicircle of office staff members and was rapidly approaching the reception desk. Despite the store manager's brisk pace, the following seconds ticked by with excruciating slowness. An eternity seemed to pass, and Kate's dread mounted almost to the unbearable stage. By the time Nathan Cordell was introduced to Joe, her throat and mouth felt dry as sawdust and her pulses were pounding. As Joe effusively pumped Nathan's hand in way of greeting, she stared at the floor, but when Nathan stepped in front of her, she had no choice except to look up at him and force her lips into a semblance of a smile. The blood rushing through her veins made such a deafening roar in her ears that she didn't really hear a word of Mr. Tilford's introduction.

Luckily, her body seemed to switch onto automatic control, and she found herself extending her right hand to Nathan. He took it firmly in his, but she managed to conceal her reaction when his fingertips grazed her palm and sent a jolt through her like a high-voltage electric shock.

"How do you do?" she said softly, evenly, not allowing herself to jerk her hand from his.

Nathan inclined his head in a brief nod, and there was not a single sign of recognition in either his expression or eyes as he looked down at her. His faint smile was merely pleasant, like one gives a stranger. The swift appraising glance that swept from the tips of her toes to the top of her head seemed as casual and unimportant as are most of the glances men give reasonably attractive females. At last, he released her hand.

"Miss Austin," was all he said, his voice as low-timbred and melodious as she remembered. He moved away.

"Well, Kate, you must not have known him very well," Joe said undiplomatically so only she could hear. "If you did, he sure didn't act like he remembered."

"No. He didn't," she murmured, at once both relieved and appalled Nathan had forgotten her completely. Once she had allowed him . . . no *longed* for him to know her more intimately than any man before or since ever had. And he had taken what she had given with such adoring eagerness. Yet now he didn't even remember her name or her face! Kate had expected at the very least a flicker of recognition to appear in his aqua eyes, but there had been no reaction whatsoever. As unobtrusively as possible, she pressed her cold fingertips to the abrupt hot ache throbbing in her right temple. At the moment she was incapable of thinking clearly. She could only feel as if she had been set adrift in a storm-tossed sea of conflicting emotions, none of them pleasant. And there was a certain little stab of sharp pain in her chest when Nathan suddenly spoke from the doorway.

"Nice meeting all of you," he said, including everyone in a collective sweeping glance. "This afternoon I'll be seeing you individually in my office. I always like to get acquainted with the staff."

With that, he left the office and Kate's stomach twisted itself into a tight knot. Encountering Nathan again within a crowd of other people was one thing. She wasn't so certain she could retain her composure when she had to see him alone later. Unadulterated dread prevented her from returning Joe's smile as he and the others drifted back to their various duties, and even her feet felt heavy as she started to return to her office.

"Too bad he's only going to be here a month or two," Molly commented as Kate passed her desk. "He's a dream, isn't he?"

"A dream," Kate repeated weakly as if she agreed, though Nathan's unexpected appearance was making her feel she had been caught up in a nightmare. After forcing a tiny smile for Molly's benefit, she stepped into her cubbyhole office, closed the door firmly behind her, and leaned wearily back against it. There she felt a little safe, although common sense told her there was no longer any place to hide.

The remainder of Kate's day was tormenting. She found it next to impossible to concentrate and could only keep her mind on her work for brief stretches of time. For hours she waited on the knife's edge of tension to be summoned by Nathan. Apparently in a gentlemanly gesture, he called in the women staff members first and when, at about three o'clock, he began seeing the men, Kate decided her name must have been accidentally omitted from his list. But if someone reminded him he hadn't yet seen her . . . The wait continued and by four thirty her nerves seemed frayed beyond repair. Her heart felt as if it literally jumped up into her throat when Molly swung the door open about ten minutes later.

"It's your turn," the receptionist blithely proclaimed, obviously not noticing the frozen expression on Kate's face. "Mr. Cordell's waiting to see you. Guess he just missed your name before." She sighed dreamily. "Wish I was just going in there. I really could look at that man all day, I think. He has the most incredible aqua eyes."

"I'd better go if he's waiting for me," Kate said hastily, getting up to rush to the door. Unwilling to hear any other young woman describe the eyes she herself had once found so fascinating, she hurried away toward the bank of elevators. Now that the moment had come, she simply wanted to get the ordeal of seeing Nathan alone over and done with. She stepped into an elevator, watched the doors glide shut, then with a muted swoosh of power, was borne up one floor. When the doors opened again, she stepped out without hesitation. Her heels sank into the deep plush of the wine carpeting that graced the corridor and reception area for the opulent executive suites. A self-induced numbness was spreading over her, and she felt strangely composed as she approached the desk.

"Oh, it's so nice to have such a good-looking man around," Jo Ann, the receptionist, said with a little giggle, tilting her head toward the west end of the building. "He's taken the offices Mr. Renaldo had, naturally. Just go on in. He's expecting you."

Kate's answering smile felt fairly natural, and she walked briskly down the long corridor to stop outside heavy oak double doors near the end. She opened one and went into the outer office, but the secretary Miss Barker was not at her desk. Kate unnecessarily smoothed her hair as she debated whether or not she should wait to be announced. If Nathan was waiting . . .

Compulsively, she went and knocked softly on the doors adjacent to the desk. Nathan's voice came back, low, muted, sending a shiver down her spine. She clenched her teeth and squared her shoulders. Six years had passed. Now Nathan was only another man, her employer of course, but nothing more than that. She opened one door to slip into the inner office, expecting to find Nathan behind his desk. He wasn't there. The coat of his charcoal gray pinstriped suit was folded neatly over the back of the leather swivel chair, and he was standing by the expansive plateglass window in his vest. The sleeves of his white shirt were rolled up to the elbows, exposing sun-bronzed muscular forearms, and Kate's eyes darkened with a hint of uncertainty while she stared at him in expectation. He continued to look out the window until she began to wonder if perhaps he hadn't heard her enter.

"Miss Barker was out," she said finally. "I thought since you were waiting, I should come in."

"I've sent her on an errand. Sit down," Nathan said flatly, turning away from the window. As she settled herself in the chair before his desk, his narrowed gaze raked over her with considerably more intensity than it had earlier. He slipped large strong hands into the pockets of his trousers and widened his stance as he surveyed her. An odd half-smile moved his mouth. "How have you been, Katie?"

No one called her Katie anymore and the sound of Nathan's deep voice saying it practically took her breath away. Yet, her expression remained deceptively serene as she met his gaze directly. "So you do remember me?" she said, keeping the sharp edge of bitterness out of her tone with great effort. "You didn't act as if you did this morning."

He raised dark eyebrows. "I didn't think you'd want anyone here to have even the slightest reason to suspect we were once . . . very close."

Direct as he had always been, he had wasted no time getting down to the basics, and Kate forced a seemingly cool impersonal smile. "You're right. People do tend to look for something to gossip about. I would rather it not be me."

"Yes, I remember how even a speculative glance in our direction used to upset you," Nathan said, coming around to sit on the edge of the desk directly in front of her. Long legs outstretched, ankles crossed, he looked perfectly relaxed, as if seeing her so unexpectedly hadn't disconcerted him one whit. "You always were a very private person and obviously the years haven't changed that any more than they've changed your appearance. You look very much the same, Katie, only now you're a beautiful woman rather than a woman-child."

"Time marches on," she responded glibly, her own gaze traveling slowly over the chiseled contours of his face. He was thirty-four now and the masculine maturity that lay over his features made him even more attractive. For several seconds she stared at him, then realized what she was doing and slowly looked away. "When I first saw you this morning, I thought you hadn't changed at all but you have. Not much but a little."

"As you say, time marches on."

22

"Yes. It's been almost six years . . ." she murmured, her voice trailing off almost pensively. Actually it was six years and two months. She had left one month before her twentieth birthday and just last month she had turned twenty-six. Would she always mark time in terms of her leaving Nathan? Her thoughts created an uncomfortable silence Nathan didn't attempt to break. His steady gaze remained riveted on her face until she felt enveloped in a cloud of nearly unbearable tension. Hot prickles spread over her skin; her entire body was suffused with oppressive heat, and although the office was air-conditioned, the atmosphere had become so stifling, she had difficulty breathing. Finally, to alleviate her own tension, she knew she must say something, anything. She made a soft little half coughing sound. "Well, the Cordell operation is really expanding, isn't it? I didn't realize until this morning that you had acquired the Barron chain."

"I preferred that the acquisition not be highly publicized."

The conversational ball was back on her side of the court too soon, but she lobbed it right back to him. "We didn't expect the president of the company to arrive here this morning. Don't they need you to run things in Charlotte?"

"The home office will manage very well until I get back. And now that we have the polite chitchat over with suppose you tell me why I haven't seen you at Evelyn's all these years," Nathan inquired brusquely, removing his hands from his pockets to cross his arms over his chest. "I expected you to visit her."

"Why would you expect that? For goodness sake, she's Phillip's mother. I'm not welcome there," Kate said, a sudden shadow of regret passing over her face. "She still blames me for what happened to Phillip, and I'm sure she still blames you. Doesn't she?"

"Yes, but I thought that because you and she were so close before Phillip died, she might have gotten over her bitterness toward you by now."

"Well, she hasn't, and I doubt she's ever going to. In fact, I'm sure she won't because every year on Phillip's birthday, I get a

23

birthday card from her, a reminder that he isn't there because of me."

"I'm sorry, Katie," Nathan murmured, leaning forward slightly. "I never would have thought Evelyn could be so unnecessarily cruel, especially since she was once so fond of you. I'd understand it better if she sent cards to me because she's always resented my family. Even after Phillip went to work at the store in Charlotte and he and I became friends, she disliked me and every other Cordell she knew. If she wants revenge so badly, why doesn't she try getting back at me?"

"Because she blames me more than you for what happened. I guess she trusted me, and I certainly betrayed that trust by spending that night with you," Kate said dully, pressing her fingertips against her forehead. "And since she's the one who told Phillip we were together, she knows why he crashed his car into that tree at Ten Oaks and killed himself."

"For God's sake, you don't still believe he crashed deliberately, do you?" Nathan asked harshly, moving with lithe swiftness to take her by the arms and haul her from the chair up before him. "Surely after six years, you must realize that the crash was an accident? Phillip was angry. He'd had a drink or two and that made him careless. He did *not* deliberately drive into that tree."

"But I'm not sure that's true!" Kate exclaimed urgently, trying in vain to escape the hard hands that held her in a binding grasp. "Evelyn told me he acted like he might do something crazy when she told him about us that night. Then he sped away in his car and . . . and . . ."

"If he wanted to kill anyone that night, it was probably me, not himself. You know as well as I do how hot-tempered he could be. He was still pretty much a kid in some ways and a reckless one at that. But he definitely wasn't suicidal."

"I just can't be as sure of that as you. I want so much to believe it was an accident, but I don't *know* that it was. All I can remember is how upset he was that afternoon when I told him

24

I wanted to break our engagement and that I was involved with someone else. I can just imagine how he must have felt when he found out it was you I was involved with." Kate's futile struggle to free herself from Nathan had ceased and her darkening gaze held his. "We were a fine pair, weren't we? You were his friend and I was his fiancée yet we . . ."

"You seem to be forgetting you broke your engagement before you spent the night with me," Nathan interrupted, the old impatience hardening his strongly carved jaw. "And I'd already ended everything with Lydia, so we weren't being unfaithful to anyone by being together. Besides, what happened between us that summer was inevitable. What we had for such a short time was wonderful and beyond what you had with Phillip. From the moment Phillip persuaded you to get a job at the store and you and I met, there was something special between us. And those weekends you and Phillip spent at Evelyn's house, when Phillip would go riding off into the distance, and we were left alone together, sharing our pasts, our dreams, our desires, just made the bond between us stronger. What happened was no one's fault. You have nothing to feel guilty about."

"Don't you feel guilty?" she questioned incredulously. "After all, when everything started, we were both engaged to other people. By the time it ended, Phillip had died, and although you went back to Lydia, she finally married someone else. Don't you feel that the two of us created a really disastrous mess?"

"I feel a regret, especially for Phillip," Nathan answered somberly, his piercing gaze bold and direct. "But I don't feel guilty."

"Maybe you don't have to now that Lydia's divorced, and you're seeing her again, according to the society page of the Charlotte paper," Kate replied flatly. "I guess it does help ease your conscience to be able to make amends. Has she forgiven you?"

"I haven't asked for forgiveness. Guilt trips are your specialty, not mine. I found that out six years ago when you tried to run away from your overworked conscience by running away from me."

"I didn't *run away*! You practically told me to go," Kate said icily, masking the hurt that came with the memory. "In fact, you did tell me to."

"Correction. I told you to either stop trying to punish yourself and me or to sew a scarlet letter on all your clothes and leave," Nathan countered caustically. "You chose to leave. You were too obsessed with your guilt and too ashamed of how much we needed each other."

"Oh yes, our great mutual need," Kate said too mockingly, her lips twisting with disdain. His need for her had been purely physical and hers for him had been . . . well, more than that but certainly physical too. "Just think how much better off everyone would have been if we'd tried to control our needs."

"How the hell do you control something as strong as what we felt?" he growled, dropping one arm down around her narrow waist to drag her close against him. His free hand slipped beneath the silken curtain of her hair at her nape, lean fingers tangling in the soft strands. "Remember how much we wanted each other, Katie, how much we needed to touch, to kiss? Until that wasn't enough for either of us anymore, and you finally stopped fighting the inevitable and me. And when we made love that night, sharing delight for hours, you said you wanted it to never end. Remember?"

"No," she lied breathlessly, appalled as her body traitorously responded to his nearness. His fingertips brushing over her scalp sent tremors up and down her spine, and the familiar male scent of his aftershave had a near dizzying effect on her senses. Oh, she remembered all right, every single glorious moment of that night they'd spent together, and now as he lowered his dark head to stroke firm lips back and forth against the softness of hers, she went stiff in his arms to keep from trembling with the intense desire she suddenly felt for him to really kiss her again. Despising herself for being weak, she turned her face aside to escape the seductively slow increasing pressure of his hard mouth. "Let me go, Nathan. Immediately."

"Time has made you even more desirable, Katie," he murmured close to her left ear, then closed his teeth gently on the tender flesh of the lobe. "And now that we're both older and more experienced, I wonder what it would be like if we made love again. Don't you?"

"No. And you're never going to find out," she retorted, nearly gasping aloud as his lips grazed the frantically beating pulse in her throat. "I'm not nineteen anymore, and we'll never make love again."

"If you're so sure of that, why is your heart pounding?" he whispered, releasing her abruptly. A disturbing sardonic smile touched his features with a certain ruthlessness and his eyes were like aqua fire as they roamed lazily over her. "Umm, Katie?"

"Don't call me that," she said coolly, managing to look much more composed than she felt. "Everyone calls me Kate now. I'd appreciate it if you did too, if you really have to call me anything at all."

"But I'm not everyone else. And I'll call you what I always have," was Nathan's flat unapologetic answer. "And rest assured that I will be calling you. Frequently, *Katie.*"

Kate's strained emotions were overwrought now and threatening to expend themselves in a volcanic outburst. She clenched her hands into tight fists at her sides as she looked at him. "You amaze me. Don't you even care what happened to Phillip?"

As Nathan loosened the knot of his burgundy tie, his hand was suddenly still. "Yes, Katie, I care very much," he said quietly. "What happened six years ago wasn't pleasant for me either."

"Then how can you even suggest that we . . . that you and I . . ."

"Phillip is part of the past," Nathan declared steadily. "We can't change any of that now and neither of us was driving the car for Phillip then. He was, too fast, too carelessly. You have to stop blaming yourself for the accident, Katie."

27

The edge of her teeth sank into the curve of her lower lip as she shook her head disappointedly. "Evelyn used to tell me that your family thought everything in the world was theirs for the taking, that they were ruthless in trying to force her to sell her farm to them. I thought she was exaggerating but now . . . Maybe she was right when she said every Cordell is born without a conscience."

Nathan took a swift step toward her. His narrowing eyes grayed to a stormy slate, always a danger signal. "Be careful what you say, Katie. You should know better than to repeat any ridiculous remark Evelyn Hughes has made. My family could have sued her for slander innumerable times, but we haven't because, frankly, we see her as a bitter pathetic woman. We don't want to add to the misery she's created for herself. But you're different. I certainly don't see you as pathetic, and I advise you to hold your tongue the next time you're tempted to make some outrageous statement about my family. I'm your employer now. Remember? I could fire you for insubordination."

"Do then," she replied coldly, swinging around to march to the door, unable to stand his mockery a moment longer. "Do whatever you please."

"Oh, I intend to. I usually do," he drawled, an irritating smile tugging at the corners of his mouth when she proudly thrust out her chin.

Only Nathan could arouse her emotions to violent intensity, and for an instant she felt the insane desire to rail at him for the hurt he had caused her in the past, for the uncertainty he was causing now. Instead, she gave him a haughty nod of her head and left his office, pulling the double doors shut firmly but quietly behind her. A moment later, when she had gained the safe haven the corridor seemed to provide, delayed reaction set in. Her head ached, and she felt as if she had been through an emotional grinder. Nathan wasn't going to make this chance encounter easy for her; she knew that. Yet what had happened between them was long past, and she wasn't a child anymore. She could handle even a man like Nathan now, she told herself. But hammering repeatedly in her mind was the old maxim: "Be careful what you wish for; you might get it." This morning she had felt the need for some excitement in her life. Now Nathan had arrived to provide that—with a vengeance.

CHAPTER TWO

Kate's thoughts were a million miles away. She stared at the couples swaying to soft music on the dance floor and heard not one word of what Joe was saying. Hoping she could stop thinking about Nathan, she had suggested they go someplace special for dinner. It wasn't working out that way. Nathan was on her mind, the image of his lean dark face was inescapable, and she was torn between trying her best to listen to Joe and memories, freshly reawakened, that would not rest again. If only Nathan hadn't touched her today, hadn't brushed her lips with his, perhaps she could have shrugged off his unexpected reappearance in her life. But he had touched and kissed her, and now she was caught up in the remembrance of how easy it had once been to surrender body and soul to him. To her, his rare combination of intelligence and raw masculinity had proved irresistible. She had believed herself in love with him then, but during the past six years she had become convinced that what she had felt had merely been infatuation. What disturbed her now was what she had learned about herself this afternoon in Nathan's office. She had discovered, to her shame, that she was still not immune to his sensuality. She was still susceptible to him, and from the moment he had touched her, she had ached to be closer to him. No lover is easily forgotten, but a first and only lover is etched indelibly in memory. And Kate was coming to the disturbing realization that Nathan had made a lasting mark on her life, a truth she had sought valiantly to ignore for years. Now she couldn't avoid reality any longer since seeing Nathan again. Unaware she was looking straight at Joe, she breathed a long tremulous sigh.

"Are you trying to bore a hole through me with your eyes?" Joe asked irritably, rousing her from her reverie. "You're staring right at me, but you've hardly listened to anything I've said all evening. What's the matter with you, Kate?"

With a murmured apology, she single-mindedly focused her attention on Joe. "I didn't mean to stare at you," she said softly. "Just wool-gathering, I guess."

"Which you've been doing all evening, in case you didn't know. Is something bothering you?"

"I've just been feeling a little restless lately," she answered, employing a half truth to avoid telling him Nathan was the real source of her agitation tonight. She lifted her shoulders in a shrug. "Maybe I just need a vacation. A couple of relaxing weeks on a sunny beach would probably do me a world of good. What do you think?"

"I think you'd better forget it while Cordell's at the store breathing down our necks," Joe stated bluntly. "Mr. Tilford says he wants everything to run like a well-oiled machine while Cordell's here, so vacations, especially for the office staff, will have to be postponed. You'll have to think of some other way to cure your restlessness."

"Maybe you can help," Kate said impulsively, slipping her hand over his where it lay on the tabletop as she gave him a sincerely affectionate smile. "I think I could feel a lot better if you'd kiss me right now."

"I'm not about to pass up a request like that," whispered Joe.

Squeezing her fingers lightly between his, he glanced around. "Even if this isn't quite the proper time or place."

Hoping against hope Joe's kiss would prove to her that any man could awaken her latent sexuality, Kate closed her eyes as he leaned toward her. She needn't have bothered. Joe's kiss, if it could be called that, was no more than a quick peck that landed on a corner of her mouth and frustrated her immensely. Her eyes slowly opened again as he sat back in his chair, but before either of them could speak, his oddly self-satisfied smile faded.

"Damn, there's Cordell and he's seen us," he muttered, putting her hand away from his. "Why did he have to be the one to see us out together? He might not approve of employees dating. Uh-oh, now he's walking this way. Suppose he'd believe this is a business dinner?"

Barely aware of Joe's question, Kate swallowed repeatedly, her mouth suddenly gone dry with the mere mention of Nathan's name. Her heartbeat accelerated to a mad pace, but she managed to take a couple of self-controlling breaths before Nathan stepped up to the small table.

"Good evening, Katie, Joe," Nathan said, his unfathomable gaze lingering on her upturned face when she reluctantly tilted her head back to look at him. As she gave him an acknowledging nod, he smiled faintly, but that smile became at once more open, less mysterious, while he accepted Joe's outstretched hand. "What a coincidence, seeing both of you here."

"Yes, sir, Kate and I were just discussing business over dinner," Joe lied. Still standing, he swept one hand toward the empty chair across the table from him. "Well, we actually haven't had dinner yet, and if you haven't, why don't you join us? Unless, of course, you've made other plans."

"No. No plans. I'm on my own tonight," Nathan replied but shook his head and gave Joe a knowing smile. "But this really doesn't look like a business dinner to me, so I wouldn't think of intruding on you and Katie."

"You wouldn't be intruding, I assure you," the younger man protested. "We'd love it if you join us. Wouldn't we, Kate?"

"Love it," she repeated dully, cutting her eyes swiftly up at Nathan when she thought she heard a low chuckle rumble up from deep in his throat. And, indeed, there was a wicked glint of amusement dancing in his eyes as they met the flash of defiance in hers. Irritated by his laughter, and by Joe for acting too much like a fawning nincompoop, she was sorely tempted to leave and let the two of them dine alone. That would have seemed as if she were running away, however, and she was unwilling to give Nathan the idea that he could intimidate her. Instead, as he sat down in the chair to her right, she gave him her most nonchalant smile. Though his knee brushed hers when he was settling himself, she didn't recoil from that unexpected physical contact. All in all, she managed to appear quite relaxed, though she didn't participate a great deal in the initial conversation. Joe immediately launched into a discussion of the store, and since Kate had wished often that he didn't make it a habit of continually talking about work, she was a bit bored.

During the meal which was soon served, however, Nathan began to steer conversation away from shoptalk and seemed to be deliberately making an effort to draw Kate into the discussion. She had forgotten what a brilliant conversationalist he could be and how knowledgeable he was in a variety of subjects. Before she knew it, she was involved in a stimulating exchange of ideas, and by the time coffee was served, she was feeling quite comfortable with Nathan.

Too comfortable, she decided abruptly when his knee accidently brushed hers once more. Knowing it would be foolhardy to truly let down her guard around him, she set about to erect a barrier between them again. She turned to Joe with a hopeful smile.

"I think I'd like to dance. I'm sure Mr. Cordell wouldn't mind if we do." She glanced at Nathan. "Would you?"

"Certainly not," he responded, a hint of amusement reappearing in his eyes. "I didn't join you to put a damper on your evening, so please enjoy yourselves."

"Well, if you really want to," Joe agreed with something less than enthusiasm as if he considered it very improper of her to suggest they dance in the presence of their new boss. He pushed back his chair. Before he could stand, a hearty slap on the back made him look up at the young man who had stopped by the table. A beaming smile spread over Joe's face. He hopped up to glance a playful blow off the newcomer's right arm. "Son of a gun, Mike Rogers! Haven't seen you since high school. What are you doing in Raleigh?"

After a few more reacquainting back-slaps, Joe asked his old friend to sit down, then introduced him to Kate and Nathan before giving her a sheepish smile. "Hope you don't mind too much if we postpone that dance, but I haven't seen old Mike here for years."

Her answering smile was understanding. "Of course I don't mind. We can dance later."

"Nonsense, Katie. You can dance now. With me," Nathan spoke up, rising from his chair and taking both her hands in his in one fluid motion. His gaze seemed to issue a challenge as he looked down at her. "Come along. I'll substitute for Joe, while he talks to his friend."

Kate pressed back in her chair and tried to discreetly withdraw her hands from his but without success. "I . . . No, thank you, Mr. Cordell," she murmured, praying he would release her. "You don't have to offer yourself as a substitute. I wasn't that eager to dance."

"But you did want to," he said firmly. "Dance with me, Katie. I insist."

Her jaw set stubbornly yet she knew if she refused Nathan now she would only succeed in arousing Joe's suspicion. Already he was staring curiously at her, as if he wondered why she simply didn't accept the kind invitation. With an inward sigh, she accepted defeat, though her glance up at Nathan was resentful as he drew her to her feet.

After being led across the dance floor to a far corner, Kate put as much distance as she possibly could between Nathan and herself, even as one large hand curved around her waist. Forcing him to hold her at arm's length was only a brief victory, as it turned out. After only a few seconds, Nathan uttered a curse beneath his breath and easily pulled her into his arms close against him.

"There," he whispered, his warm breath stirring a tendril of her hair. "That's better, isn't it?"

She stiffly shook her head. "I don't happen to think so."

"Don't be ridiculous. I'm not carrying any communicable diseases, so just relax."

Doing that was virtually impossible, considering Nathan's proximity. As he and Kate moved together in time with the music, his tautly muscled thighs rubbed lightly against the slender length of hers, and when he slipped both arms around her, crossing his wrists at the small of her back, a shiver of awareness danced over her skin. Desperate to steel herself to the disruptive effect of his nearness, she was actually relieved when he spoke and diverted her attention.

"You and Joe are more than just coworkers," he stated rather than asked. "Is it serious? Since you aren't wearing a ring, I assume you're not engaged."

"Not officially," she responded stiffly. "We've talked about getting married."

"You shouldn't marry him, Katie," Nathan announced calmly. "He's as wrong for you as Phillip was."

Indignation sent hot color rising in her cheeks. Tensing, she counted to ten before muttering frigidly, "You're the last person who should try to tell me who's right or wrong for me. At least Phillip wanted to marry me and Joe does too. That's more than you ever wanted to do."

A hand came up to curve the back of her head, tilting it back so she was forced to meet Nathan's dark intent gaze. "Katie, you weren't ready for that kind of commitment and you know it. You wanted to finish college. And you weren't even twenty yet," he said, his voice low, his tone uneven. "You were too young for marriage."

"Oh, come on, you can think of a better excuse than that," she taunted. "I was too young for marriage. But *not* too young to take to bed?"

"Too young for that too," he answered, his expression both disturbed and disturbing. "But I had to have you that night, Katie. I couldn't keep my hands off you, and it just happened. I couldn't fight it and neither could you."

Kate's breath caught deep in her throat as the strange light that suddenly flared in the depths of his aqua eyes became almost mesmerizing. Horrified that she might fall under the spell of that calculatedly tender gaze he had always employed in the past to seduce her, she riveted her attention on the strong brown column of his neck where it extended up from his crisp shirt collar. "I don't want to talk about this anymore," she said curtly. "I don't need anyone, least of all you, giving me advice about men."

"I disagree. But your wish is my command," he drawled, pressing her even closer to him. "I won't mention Joe or Phillip again. Tonight anyway."

If he was trying to bait her, he was doing an excellent job, but Kate refused to be lured into a war of words she probably couldn't win because she would be angry and he wouldn't be. Cooler heads invariably triumph in a debate even if the logic is flawed, and Kate knew that even if there was a slim hope of her winning she needed to shore up her defenses against Nathan before entering into a full-fledged argument. Remaining silent, she followed easily as he guided her around the dance floor but breathed an inner sigh of relief when the band stopped playing for a moment.

"Thank you for the dance," she said primly, starting to move in the direction of their table. "But we'd better get back before Joe thinks we've deserted him."

"Better give him more time with his friend," Nathan suggested, catching her arm to halt her progress midstride. "They seemed to have a great deal they wanted to talk about."

"But . . ." Kate began then abandoned the attempted protest as Nathan gracefully swung her back into his arms when the music started again. This time the tempo was slower, more lazily romantic, and resigned to one more dance, she gradually allowed herself to move in perfect unison with Nathan, in time to the softly throbbing sensuous beat. Nathan was an exceptional dancer, moving with natural, easy rhythm. She couldn't have denied that dancing with him was a pleasurable experience. His arms were crossed around her lower back. His hands warmed her waist through the sheer georgette fabric of her blouse, and becoming caught up in the mood the music was creating, she moved her own shapely arms up from between them to drape them across his broad shoulders. Even when Nathan lifted her hair away from her neck and bent down to graze his lips over creamy satin skin near her nape, she couldn't resist. The rush of delight that swept through her was too warmly pleasurable. Her head fell back slightly against his supporting hand, exposing the length of gently curved neck to the searching brushing touch of his mouth.

"*Katie,*" he whispered huskily, the arm still around her waist tightening.

It was the unmistakable stirring of aroused masculinity surging strongly against her thighs that brought her to her senses. The touch of his lips created no more pleasure, only emotional pain. With an urgent muffled protest, Kate pushed away from him. "I don't want to dance anymore," she muttered. "I'm going back to the table."

Making no attempt to stop her this time, Nathan followed across the dance floor, then gallantly held her chair as she sat down. Unable to force herself to murmur thanks, she merely

37

gave him a hard cold glance before turning toward Joe. He was so involved in conversation with his friend, Mike, that at last she had to touch his arm to gain his attention.

"Would you take me home now?" she asked softly. "I'm really sorry to break up the party but . . . I'm feeling rather tired."

For a fraction of a second, indecision was written on Joe's face as chivalry warred with his desire to stay with his old friend. Finally he shrugged. "Sure, I'll take you home. Mike, you wouldn't mind waiting here until I can get back, would you?"

"Oh, that's not necessary. I can save you a trip by driving Katie home for you," Nathan interceded with an innocent smile. "I'd be happy to do it."

"*No.* I mean, that would be too inconvenient for you, Mr. Cordell," Kate said hastily. "If Joe wants to spend more time with Mike, I don't mind staying here. I'm not really all that tired."

"Mike has to leave Raleigh tomorrow, so we have a lot of catching up to do tonight. All our reminiscing would probably only bore you, Kate." Joe smiled at her and absently patted her hand. "So if you're tired and Mr. Cordell doesn't mind driving you home, you'd probably be happier if you went."

Kate could easily have murdered him. She stared at him incredulously, but before she could open her mouth to say a word, Nathan was on his feet and taking her arm to draw her up out of her own chair.

"That's settled then. I'll drive you home, Katie. And it's no inconvenience," he said with an unabashed smile though she glowered up at him.

"Thanks, Mr. Cordell. See you tomorrow, Kate," said Joe before turning back to his friend.

Deadly silent, Kate allowed Nathan to place her crocheted shawl around her shoulders then preceded him at a brisk pace past the station where the maitre d' stood. She stopped, however, when Nathan caught one elbow and halted to remove his wallet from his pocket. "Please tell the gentleman at table six that the bill has been taken care of," he instructed, handing the man some folded bills.

A moment later, when Nathan opened one of the double stained-glass doors for Kate, and she stepped out onto the canopied walkway in the cool night air, she wrapped her shawl snugly around her, more a protective gesture than an attempt to keep warm. She and Nathan said nothing to each other while waiting for his car to be brought around. After he helped her into his silver Jaguar sedan then lowered himself into the driver's seat, she tried to relax, no easy accomplishment while confined in the luxurious but small space of the car with him. Watching out of the corner of her eye as he turned the key in the ignition to start the powerful engine, she expected him to ask for directions to her house. He didn't. With one lean hand on the steering wheel, he swung the Jaguar south on Glenwood.

"Good guess. You're going in the right direction," Kate commented. "I live on . . ."

"Hillsborough Street," he provided dryly. "West. Right?"

"Yes," Kate said, eyeing him warily. "But how did you know that?"

"Your address was in your personnel file. And I have an excellent memory."

"Oh. I see. Well, do you know how to get to Hillsborough Street from here?"

"Right at the next stoplight, isn't it?" He glanced sideways at her and smiled lightly when she nodded. "I thought I remembered the way. I'm guessing your apartment is probably just beyond the Peace College campus, and I had a date once with a girl who went to Peace."

"Not surprising," Kate retorted tartly. "You've probably dated at least one girl at every college in the state."

"Not quite," Nathan said, laughing easily despite the obvious sarcasm in her comment. "I have to admit, though, that I gave it my best shot during my undergraduate years at Carolina. But since you brought up the subject of dating habits, I have to tell you that you seem to make a habit of choosing young men who willingly hand you over to me. First, Phillip did it. And tonight Joe. Wonder why your boyfriends find it so easy to trust you with me?"

Glaring at the carved profile silhouetted in the soft glow of the dashlights, Kate muttered, "Maybe they just aren't very good at recognizing a wolf in sheep's clothing."

"By that, I imagine you're referring to me?" Nathan shook his head. "No, Katie, I don't think it has anything to do with me. It's just that your young men feel they can trust you completely."

"Well, Phillip certainly discovered I wasn't trustworthy, didn't he?" Kate said, her voice slightly strained.

"That's not true, Katie," Nathan gently admonished her.

"Oh, yes, it is." Leaning forward in her seat as Nathan drove past the campus with its huge old shade trees and vintage stone buildings, Kate pointed straight ahead. "You see that brick building about two blocks down? That's it." Sitting back again, she felt pleased with herself for adroitly nipping that disturbing conversation in the bud. And when Nathan maneuvered the car into a tight parking space on the street across from her building, she was highly relieved that this interminable evening was finally ending. In only a few minutes, she would be able to escape Nathan and everything else by seeking the sanctuary of her small but gloriously private apartment.

Nathan, however, had other ideas. After taking her key to unlock the door of her second-floor apartment, he glanced in at her neat living room then looked down at her expectantly. "Nice place. Aren't you going to invite me in?"

Though her heart seemed to do a crazy little somersault, Kate masked her sudden intense uneasiness by maintaining a cool, almost indifferent, expression as she shrugged slightly. "Sure. Come in. Would you care for a drink? I don't have a well-stocked bar, but I believe I do have rum and Scotch."

"Then we're in luck. I'll have Scotch. With water, if you don't remember," Nathan told her while surveying with interest the painting that hung above her sofa. "I like this. Know the artist?"

"Yes and so do you. Joe painted that," she said with a supremely satisfied smile. "Talented, isn't he?"

"Very." Stroking the strong line of his jaw with one finger, Nathan examined the painting more carefully. "Considering his artistic ability, I'm surprised he chose personnel management as his career. Why not something more suitable to his talent?"

"I asked him that. He said he didn't want to be another starving artist, so he decided to choose a career that would earn him some money. Painting had to become a hobby."

"Pity. But I suppose talent alone doesn't assure success," Nathan said, adding a thank you when she came across the room to hand him his drink. "An artist has to also be dedicated, persistent, and willing to make a few sacrifices if he wants art to be his life's work."

"If you're insinuating Joe is lazy, I can assure you he isn't," Kate said, her words clipped. Sitting down on the edge of the sofa, she indicated with a sweeping movement of one hand that he should also take a seat. "You'll soon discover that he works very hard managing the store's personnel department."

Nathan shook his head, watching her over the rim of the glass he raised to his lips. "Don't be so defensive, Katie. I wasn't insinuating Joe is lazy," he said after taking a slow sip of his drink. "I was merely stating what is obviously a fact—Joe doesn't feel a driving need to be an artist. I wasn't insulting him. In fact, I like him. He's a pleasant young man."

"Yes, he is," said Kate, slightly mollified. "Actually, he's one of the most pleasant men I've ever met."

"Maybe so," Nathan conceded with a blasé shrug. "But he's still not right for you."

A tiny frown appeared with lightning speed on Kate's brow, and she clenched her hands together in her lap. "I've already told you I'd appreciate you keeping your opinion about that to yourself," she pronounced tersely, her expression indignant. "You are my employer now but that hardly gives you the right to evaluate my personal relationships."

Nathan shrugged again, apparently with a total lack of concern this time. Relaxing back on the sofa, he proceeded to remove his tie, fold it neatly, and slip it into a pocket of his coat. As he undid his collar button, he stretched his legs, assuming a thoroughly relaxed posture that seemed to indicate he planned to stay awhile.

The silence that hovered between them became increasingly uncomfortable for Kate as the minutes passed. Frequently, she glanced at Nathan's glass but the amber liquid it contained wasn't disappearing very fast. She began to wonder if he was ever going to stop nursing that drink and leave so she could start to unwind from what had been the most nerve-wracking day she had spent in six years.

"Katie, if you're planning to get up and do something, then do it," Nathan told her a minute or so later. "If not, sit back and relax. You're poised on the edge of that cushion as if you're about to sprout wings and take flight."

Kate immediately slipped back on the sofa, her fingers busily straightening the soft folds of her black crepe de chine skirt. Unwilling to endure another prolonged silence, she said the first thing that popped into her mind. "How are your parents? I read about your father's retirement. I hope he's enjoying it."

"Both he and Mother are having a terrific time. They travel a great deal. Right now they're wandering around Europe. And your parents? How are they?"

Kate smiled fondly. "They're fine too. And how's your sister, Jean? Had any more children?"

"Two more. And they're all fine." After putting his glass down on the table in front of him, Nathan suddenly moved with the awesome swiftness of a pouncing panther close to Kate's side. He lightly gripped her chin between thumb and forefinger. "Enough of this. We can talk about our families later. Right now, I want . . ."

His words broke off as he proceeded to demonstrate exactly what it was he did want. Before Kate could even try to resist, his mouth was on her own, moving with slow brushing strokes, his touch tormentingly light.

Momentarily too stunned to react, Kate sat immobile until Nathan's hard-carved lips began to communicate an overwhelming passion that was slowly but surely arousing a similar response in her. She panicked. With a muffled little cry, she threw her hands against his chest only to have them both caught in one of his. Subduing her resistance with astonishingly little physical effort, he pressed her hands back against her, his own hard knuckles sinking with compelling pressure into the yielding cushioned flesh of her breasts. A razor-sharp thrill shot through her, dizzying in its intensity, and suddenly Kate could no longer deny herself the heightening pleasure of his kiss. She kissed him back, her mouth opening slightly, inviting the invasion of the tip of the tongue that tasted her own. She softly moaned, and taking her response as acquiescence, Nathan released her hands. They went back against his chest, but this time to stroke in small circular motions over the taut muscular contours and to linger with feathery caresses on the hardening nubs of flat nipples outlined against the fabric of his shirt.

With a low deep groan, Nathan swiftly gathered her to him and sat back, bringing her into his arms and across his muscular thighs. As he cradled her against him, their kiss deepened. His lips hardened with a hungry desire to plunder the softness of hers, and his teeth closed gently on the tender lower curve, opening her mouth wider beneath the onslaught of his. His warm minty breath filled her throat, and as she eagerly pressed herself closer, he enfolded her in a tighter, more relentless embrace.

Lost in the ravishing power of his possessive kiss, Kate couldn't think. She was alive with primitive sensations that welled up from the very core of her being, and she could only feel the quickening piercing need a woman feels for a particular man. Since Nathan, no other man had ever made her feel this

43

way, and she was caught up in the dreamlike recollection of the night they had made love for hours and the ecstasy of the long slow thrusts of his hardness inside her. Remembering, she trembled and a central emptiness bloomed deep within her and clamored to be filled. Molding the soft curves of her slight body to the firmer masculine line of his, she caressed his neck with feverish hands then dropped one down to knead the corded muscles of his shoulders while the fingers of the other tangled urgently in his thick vibrant hair. Nathan's lips exerted a gentle twisting pressure on hers until they clung hungrily to his. Her passion was rising to match his own now, and even his low murmur of triumph didn't lessen the need for him she felt.

Kate watched through half-closed eyes when Nathan lifted his head and a hand over one hipbone pressed her back until she was lying in his lap. A rush of anticipated pleasure raced hotly through her veins as he slowly unfastened the tiny buttons of her blouse. His mouth sought the scented hollow at the base of her throat. His teeth nipped at sensitized skin that stretched with taut smoothness over her collarbone. Feathering searing little kisses downward, he pressed his lips into the shadowed valley between full firm breasts and the tip of his tongue explored the satin texture of her skin.

It was a caress that had never failed to arouse her. Erotic delight evoked a spreading warmth that weakened her lower limbs, and realizing she would soon be on the very edge of total surrender, she heeded the final weak cry of warning from her common sense. More afraid of herself than of Nathan, she shook her head slowly back and forth in the crook of his supporting arm. "No. Don't do that," she breathed. "Stop."

He didn't. His lips explored every inch of the swelling curves of her breasts exposed above the top of her lace-edged camisole, his touch and his breath burning her skin. "You don't want me to stop, Katie," he murmured back. "You used to want me to do this."

"As you said, I was too young to know what I wanted then."

44

A certain darkness shadowed the fiery glint of passion in Nathan's eyes as he lifted his head to look down at her. "If you felt that way, maybe you wish the statutory rape law extended to age twenty-one. Then you could have pressed charges against me."

Astonished by the mere suggestion, Kate hastily shook her head. "I couldn't have done that, Nathan. I've never tried to pretend that what happened was your fault. It wasn't rape in any way. I knew what I was doing."

"But you just said you didn't know what you wanted then."

"But I meant . . . Oh, I don't know what I meant. You twist my words around so much that even I'm not sure anymore what I'm saying."

"What you wanted then doesn't matter anyway. All that counts is what you want right now," he whispered huskily, slipping her blouse and the straps of her camisole off her shoulders down her arms. A muscle ticked in his jaw as he gazed down at the rapid rise and fall of her partially covered breasts, and he cupped their weight in his gently squeezing hands. "Tell me, Katie. What do you want me to do? Shall I go on touching you? Or shall I stop?"

His hands dropped, and Kate gasped at the nearly unbearable sense of loss she felt. Her entire body throbbed achingly for his caresses, and with an agonized moan of defeat, she caught his hands in her own to bring them back up and press them down harder into the pillowed softness of her breasts. They swelled to his touch that scorched her skin even through the lace cups of her bra, and when he slipped his hands beneath the flimsy fabric to gently rub the straining rose-tipped peaks between his fingers, the shattering desire that shafted through her was too strong and primitive to resist. He had won. She wrapped her arms around him as his masterful lips took the softness of hers again and again in long dangerously deepening kisses that soon induced in her total acquiescence. She explored his long hard body with caressing hands while he slowly drew her skirt down past her hips, to drop silently to the floor. His hands roamed over the rounded curve of feminine hips, the enticing insweep of her waist, and the rounded flesh of her breasts. Afloat in the sensuous pleasures they were sharing, Kate slipped her hands inside his shirt, delighting in the taut smoothness of his heated skin. She wanted to go on touching him forever as Nathan slipped a hand between her shapely thighs, grazing it upward. His fingertips drifted lightly against her most secret feminine warmth, sending a violent tremor over her.

"God, I need you, Katie," he groaned. "Tell me where your bedroom is."

One small hand moved in the direction of a closed door across the room. "Over there," she whispered, her breathing quickening as he swiftly stood with her in arms. Even as she burrowed her face against the curve of his neck, she was overcome by the unbidden memory of the other night she had spent with him. At least then he had uttered the lie and told her he loved her. Tonight he hadn't even done that, and she was suddenly terrified she would hate herself tomorrow if she surrendered to him now. To her eternal shame, she longed to make love with him, yet she was wise enough to realize her self-respect was worth far more than a few hours of physical gratification. Desire ebbed away as Nathan carried her toward her room, and before he reached the door, she went stiff in his arms.

"Please put me down," she said firmly, her expression adamant when he looked down at her face. "This has gotten completely out of hand. I know I've given you the idea I'm willing to . . . But I'm not. Not now, not ever. Just put me down and leave now, Nathan."

Ominously silent, he lowered her feet to the floor and watched as she hastily gathered her camisole back up around her. A semblance of a smile touched his hard mouth. "You've learned how to play very rough, Katie," he muttered cuttingly. "But if you think acting the tease will discourage me, you're wrong. We've begun a game I intend to ultimately win."

"But why?" she exclaimed heatedly, slapping back a strand of hair. Reproach-darkened eyes searched his lean face, but she could only see an unrelenting ruthlessness sharpening his features. "What do you want from me, Nathan? Do you get some kind of thrill out of reconquering former conquests?"

"Something like that," was his blunt reply. Turning, he strode toward the door but stopped before he reached it to look back. "Remember, Katie, our game's just beginning, and we're going to play it out to the very end."

"This *is* the end!" she shot back, but before the last word was out of her mouth, he was pulling the door shut behind him, leaving her alone with only the hollow sound of her own voice. Out in the hallway, his footsteps receded to silence and Kate suppressed an urge to hurl something breakable at the door and raked her fingers through her hair instead. With a gutteral cry of pure frustration, she threw herself onto the sofa, curling up into a tight little ball in one corner. Wrapping her arms around her drawn-up legs, she rested her forehead on her knees while bitterly berating herself for what she had allowed to happen this evening. It had been stupid enough to allow him to drive her home but to invite him in had been the height of insanity. Yet, she had truly believed she could handle him but that was before she had known he was determined to play this potentially devastating little game of his. Now that she knew the truth, however, she could strengthen her defenses against him. She would never allow herself to be vulnerable where he was concerned again. She was a strong-willed woman, and she could resist Nathan. Unless she was willing to let him use her again, she had to. He was going to discover that this was one game he couldn't possibly win, she told herself repeatedly. But as she tiredly nuzzled her head against the back of the sofa, her heart was suddenly afraid.

CHAPTER THREE

During the week that followed, Kate saw Nathan only a few times and then only from a distance. Much to her relief, he didn't seek her out, and she certainly didn't go looking for him. By sticking as closely as she could to her office, she lessened the chances of bumping into him, and after a few days had passed, the memory of what had happened in her apartment faded to some extent. The niggling little fear that had been born that night became far less persistent until she was almost at the point of deciding that she had overreacted to Nathan's threat about playing a game he planned to win. It was more likely that he had simply hoped she would obligingly provide him with a convenient one-night stand, but because she had refused to satisfy his need for casual sex, he probably hadn't given her another thought since. After all, he could find plenty of women far more cooperative than Kate had been. Wealthy, virilely handsome, and nearly irresistibly charming when he chose to be, he had always drawn females like a magnet. This was a fact Kate had been well aware of six years ago, and the way the women of the office staff had swooned over him the past week had merely served to remind her that he would never suffer the lack of female companionship. A reassuring thought. With many other women at his beck and call, he wouldn't want to bother with her.

By Thursday Kate had managed, more or less, to banish Nathan from her thoughts. Out of sight, out of mind, she thought with a rueful inward smile as she methodically arranged some personnel files on her desk. Her smile faded, however, when Molly rang her to announce that Mr. Nathan Cordell himself wished to see her in his office immediately.

"Did . . . his secretary mention why he wants to see me?" Kate almost whispered into the receiver, hoping she didn't sound nearly as breathless as she suddenly felt. "Am I supposed to bring anything up to his office with me?"

"She didn't say," Molly informed her. "All she said was that Mr. Cordell wants to see you immediately."

"Right this minute?"

"She said he's expecting you. Gosh, Kate, you sound like you'd rather not go up to see him. That's crazy. I just wish he'd call me in once in a while. I'd be in his office so fast, it'd make your head swim."

Kate had to smile, even as she compulsively tucked a wayward wisp of hair back into the loose chignon on her nape. Taking herself in hand, she breathed deeply, thereby easing some of the unreasonable anxiety she felt. In her most professional tone, she instructed Molly to inform Nathan's secretary that she was on her way to see him. After replacing the receiver, she got up from her desk, squaring her shoulders while smoothing the skirt of her navy suit. Head held high, she then proceeded out of her office.

A moment later, when the elevator doors glided open, Kate was nearly run down by Joe, who rushed out as she waited to step in. She could see something had happened to upset him. His face was flushed a dark crimson color and his lips were pressed tightly together, grimly set.

"Joe! What's the matter?" she exclaimed, touching his arm then staring bewilderedly at him when he practically flung her hand away. Unconsciously, she took a step back from him.

49

Unadulterated fury seemed to emanate from him, and she couldn't possibly imagine what could have happened to make him as angry as this. She gestured helplessly. "Please tell me what's wrong. You look so upset. Tell me what . . ."

"You're on your way up to see Cordell, right? Then you'll find out what's happened soon enough, I guess," Joe muttered between clenched teeth. "I'll let him tell you."

"*Tell me what?*" A sudden horrible thought struck Kate, and her face went slightly pale. "Oh, Joe, you can't have been fired?"

Joe sneered. "No, I haven't been fired," he answered shortly, cold eyes flicking over her. "Actually, all this concerns you."

"*Me?*" Kate's cheeks went whiter still and she felt rather ill. If Nathan had taken it upon himself to tell Joe about their relationship years ago, no wonder Joe was upset. Yet, surely even Nathan couldn't do something so horrid! Although she hoped that he couldn't have with all her heart, she had to be certain. Her voice sounded somewhat strangled as she asked, "Are you saying this . . . concerns me personally?"

"Well, of course not! How could it? Cordell's our boss, nothing more," Joe snapped, tightening the knot of his tie with a jerk that was almost violent. "There's nothing personal about this little mess. I'd bet my last dollar it's just another case of office politics."

Kate was now thoroughly confused. "Then, what *is* going on? For goodness sake, what exactly are you talking about? Office politics?"

"As I said, I'll let the 'big man' tell you," Joe mumbled. Twisting around on one heel, he then walked away from her, his rapid gait and noisy footfalls on the marble floor leaving little doubt as to the extent of his agitation.

A concerned perplexed frown marred Kate's porcelain smooth brow as she watched him march away. Absently she stepped onto the elevator, and as the doors swept shut behind her, another horrible unbidden thought ricocheted through her brain. A case of office politics, Joe had said, yet he had admitted he hadn't been fired. But what if he knew *she* was about to be and simply hadn't had the heart to tell her? Kate's heart seemed to sink down into the center of her stomach, and she slowly shook her head. Surely Nathan couldn't be so vindictive simply because she had refused to surrender to his advances the other night? Or could he be?

Tormented by a relentless feeling of uncertainty, Kate left the elevator to walk woodenly along the corridor toward Nathan's suite of offices. Mounting apprehension dragged at her legs, making them feel almost too heavy to move. Six years she had worked at Renaldo's, at first only part-time as a clerk. But as the years had passed, she had been consistently rewarded with additional responsibilities, and she was rather proud of the position she held now. Six years and she had only occasionally even considered leaving Renaldo's, but if Nathan fired her, she would have to leave. And if he refused to provide her with an honest favorable reference, she might have very little chance of securing a comparable position elsewhere.

Kate's stomach was churning when she opened the door and entered his secretary's office and that physical manifestation of her emotional state didn't abate one bit when the woman looked up from her desk, her expression stony. Miss Barker, a diminutive woman with a cap of pure white hair, had been employed at Renaldo's since the dawning of time, and though she had always been genuinely friendly to Kate, she didn't offer so much as a smile to her today.

"Mr. Cordell expected you about five minutes ago," she declared flatly with a toss of a hand toward the door adjacent to her desk. "You'd better get right in there."

Nodding, Kate forced a swallow past the rapidly expanding lump in her throat. Almost in a self-protective trance, she went to knock once on Nathan's door, then went in. Once again, he was coatless and the sleeves of his white shirt were pushed up almost to his elbows. He appeared very busy and didn't look up from the sheaf of papers he held in his right hand.

"Sit down, Katie," he commanded matter-of-factly, finally laying the papers aside as she took the chair before his desk. He looked up at her, his eyes neither warmly blue or coldly green but something in between—perhaps cobalt like a sky in which a storm is gathering.

Too proud to look away, Kate met his intent gaze squarely, though her hands were clenched tightly together in her lap. A forced semblance of a questioning smile touched her lips but just barely.

"I have a proposition for you, Katie," Nathan announced abruptly, leaning back in his swivel chair and clasping his hands behind the back of his head as he continued to survey her closely. "I think you'll be very interested in it. I imagine you remember Betty Warner, our assistant personnel director in our home office in Charlotte? She's decided to take an early retirement, and I called you to offer you her position."

Kate's relief was nearly dizzying in its intensity. Before she could prevent herself, she released her breath in an audible sigh. Tension diminished and astonishment took its place. Her eyes widened as she stared at Nathan, and suddenly she was afraid to really believe what he had said. "Are you being serious?" she asked somewhat skeptically. "Or is this just some kind of joke at my expense?"

"I never joke around when it comes to business," was his quick answer. "And you know me well enough to realize that. Now, are you interested in the offer or not? I'm sure you're aware that it would be a great advance in your career to go from being an assistant personnel director in one store to become the assistant personnel director of the entire chain. Betty's decision to retire early has presented you with a once-in-a-lifetime opportunity. Wouldn't you agree?"

Kate nodded as excitement increased the tempo of her heartbeat and coursed invigoratingly through her veins. Nathan was right. This was a rare opportunity, and she could scarcely believe he was giving her, of all people, the chance to take advantage of it. Pressing one hand palm downward against her chest, she shook her head bemusedly. "But why me, Nathan?" she asked, forgetting momentarily that such a question wasn't exactly self-assured and professional. It was simply honest, and she didn't attempt to retract it. "I guess I don't understand why you're offering the position to me when there must be personnel directors in every store you own who have more experience than I do."

"Ah, but that's to your advantage in this situation. I, personally, want someone young in this position, someone who won't feel compelled by age to leave Cordell's to become the director of personnel elsewhere. You're young enough to be patient until Gary Roberts retires as director in ten years or so. Then you can step into his position while you're still in your midthirties. I'd call that making a success of your career. After being Gary's assistant for ten or twelve years, you'd be well qualified to take his place."

"You really are serious about this, aren't you?" she asked, leaning forward in her chair, unable to conceal the amazement in her soft voice. When Nathan smiled faintly and nodded, her excitement bubbled up to overflowing. "Oh, Nathan, this is really wonderful. I can hardly believe it; it's such a terrific opportunity."

Watching her closely, he was silent for a moment. Then he nodded. "I assume that means you're accepting the position?"

"Well, of course I am! How could I not? I'd have to be a nitwit not . . ." Her voice trailed off abruptly as a sudden twinge of guilt pulled at her conscience. A tiny little frown appeared on her brow, and she lifted her hand in an uncertain gesture. "Wait a minute; I'm confused again. Why didn't you offer this position to Joe? He's only two years older than me, and since he is personnel director here, he seems to be a more suitable candidate than I am."

"Seems to be doesn't mean he is," Nathan said flatly, hooking his thumbs into the shallow pockets of his vest. "I've seen your personnel file and his and, frankly, you should be personnel director instead of him. You have more retail experience than he does. He only has two years; you have six, and although you weren't in management all that time, you were still gaining retail experience he doesn't have. In my judgment, that makes you more qualified." He regarded her somberly. "Why were you passed over for the position of director last year? Why was Joe given the promotion?"

Kate wrinkled her nose. "The truth of the matter is that Mr. Renaldo had some very old-fashioned ideas, one of which was that women should be the subordinates of men. It could never be the other way around."

Nathan's darkly slashed brows lifted. "I'm surprised you tolerated such a sexist attitude. Didn't you think of resigning in protest?"

"I did think of it. And if you hadn't offered me the position you did today, I probably would have left Renaldo's eventually." Kate shrugged resignedly. "I have to admit I did feel resentful because I'd been passed over for the position."

"Resentment toward Joe?"

"No." Kate was taken aback. "It was Mr. Renaldo's decision, his mistake. It really wouldn't have been very fair of me to resent Joe for taking the position when it was offered to him."

Nathan's eyes narrowed. He leaned forward to rest his folded arms on the desktop. "And how do you think Joe's going to react about your being promoted to a position above him now? Will he resent only me? Or will his resentment include you too?"

"Oh, no, I'm sure it won't. He'll be pleased for me," Kate answered automatically before stopping to think clearly. Then she fell silent. Catching her upper lip between her teeth she stared at her hands in her lap for several long seconds as she recalled the foul mood Joe had been in when they had met at the elevator. Some of the joyous edge went off her excitement. She looked up at Nathan. "You've already told Joe you were going to offer the position to me, haven't you?"

"I felt I owed him that. Under the circumstances, I knew he might be surprised he wasn't offered the job."

"Surprised and rather upset, judging by the way he was acting when I saw him just before coming up here."

When Kate sighed, Nathan got up, came around the desk, and stood beside her chair, hands in his pockets as he looked down at her. "And you still think Joe won't resent you for accepting the position? Even though it does mean, of course, a transfer to Charlotte?"

Confusion momentarily shadowed Kate's face. Charlotte was where Nathan lived, and the home office was where he worked most of the time. If she accepted this promotion, she might possibly be seeing him on almost a daily basis, a disturbing prospect, because deep in her heart, she was afraid she could be foolish enough to drift into another intimate involvement with him. Yet, a person cannot run away from a fear forever. There comes the time when even the most frightening aspect of life must be faced head on, then defeated. And Kate felt this might very well be her time to defeat the lingering remnants of her attraction to Nathan. She was old enough and wise enough now to keep her relationship with him on a strictly professional basis. Simply because she moved to Charlotte and came in contact with him fairly frequently didn't mean she had to become personally involved with him. She just would not allow that to happen.

Such firm resolve bolstered her confidence although she hadn't forgotten she still had the problem with Joe to face. He wouldn't be at all pleased to learn she had decided to transfer to Charlotte, and she really couldn't blame him for that. What they needed to do in this situation was to sit down together and discuss it thoroughly. All these thoughts raced through her brain in only a few seconds, and in actuality she just hesitated briefly before responding to Nathan's question about Joe's reaction.

"I guess I'd better go find him," she said softly, rising from her chair. "We have a lot to talk about."

When Kate started to step by Nathan, he reached out without

warning to lay his hands heavily on her shoulders. "Don't be too disappointed if he puts some of the blame for this situation on you."

Gazing up into his tanned face with its finely carved features, Kate shook her head. "I'm sure he won't be so unfair, and I think I can make him understand what I have to do."

"Your decision's firm then?" Nathan questioned, regarding her with a certain quiet concentration that seemed almost an attempt to search out the very essence of her being. "You definitely want the position in the home office?"

"Yes. I want it," she replied, thinking for an infinitesimal instant that her answer had brought a triumphant glint to his eyes. Yet the impression was so fleeting she thought she must have imagined seeing such a response, and when he removed his hands from her shoulders, she paused only a second before turning and leaving his office.

Kate found Joe in the staff breakroom ten minutes later. Sitting at one of the two formica-topped tables, he was staring dolefully at the coffee he was swirling in a paper cup. If he heard Kate enter, he gave no indication of it and seemed mesmerized by the tiny whirlpool he was creating. His elbows were resting on the tabletop. His expression was morose and his shoulders hunched, and Kate sighed inwardly as she went across the room to the counter where the new automatic drip coffee maker had been placed. After pouring a cup of the steaming dark brown liquid, she added sugar then joined Joe at the table.

Unable to ignore her any longer, he glanced up, and the petulant look that came over his face made her think rather uncharitably that he looked like a child who had just been denied candy. Yet she gave him a tentatively hopeful smile. "I know you know about the offer," she said softly. "And I'm sorry if you're upset."

"*If I'm upset!* Oh, I'm upset all right," Joe snapped, putting his cup down so hard that the contents sloshed up and out over his hand which caused him to utter a loud oath of frustration. Yanking a paper napkin from a metal holder, he meticulously dried his skin, all the while muttering to himself. Then he turned his full attention to Kate again. "Don't you think I have good reason to be mad enough to chew nails? After all, I'm your superior here, but I've been passed over and *you've* been offered the job in the home office. That promotion should have been mine and you know it, Kate."

She frowned slightly. "Well, it's really not all that simple, Joe."

"The hell it isn't! I'm the personnel director here and you're only my assistant, and it sure doesn't make sense that you were offered the position instead of me."

"You seem to be forgetting I have more experience in the retail business than you do," she remarked calmly though her frown did deepen. "But that didn't stop Mr. Renaldo from passing me over and promoting you last year."

"Oh, that's altogether different," Joe retorted impatiently, with a dismissive toss of one hand. "He had a valid reason for doing what he did. After all, I'm a man."

"And what in the world does that have to do with anything?" Kate visibly bristled but by silently counting to ten managed to control her temper, though she was still far from pleased with Joe's inane ridiculous comment. Unknowingly strumming her fingertips on the tabletop, she stared at him. "Since you are upset, I'm going to pretend you never said anything so preposterous. I'm sure you didn't really mean it."

"Didn't I?" Joe replied heatedly then relented and lowered sheepish eyes. "All, right, I guess I didn't. But I still think I should have been offered the position in Charlotte before you. I'm not going to enjoy knowing I was second choice."

Kate's patience was already growing thin, and she was in no mood to be confused by nonsensical statements. She moved restlessly in her chair. "What do you mean about not enjoying being second choice? I really have no idea what you're talking about. Second choice for what?"

"Assistant personnel director at the home office. What else?"

Joe asked irritably. "Cordell's almost certainly going to offer the position to me since you've turned it down."

Kate's eyes widened disbelievingly. "But, Joe, I haven't turned the job down."

"We both know you're going to, though," he proclaimed too self-assuredly. "You certainly wouldn't seriously consider accepting it."

Speechless with amazement for several seconds, she could only move her mouth soundlessly and shake her head at him. At last she found her voice and said tersely, "I can't imagine why you'd think I wouldn't happily seize such a great opportunity. That would be sheer madness. And I've already accepted the offer."

Joe stiffened. His face flushed an angry red. "You've what? How could you do that to me? Don't you realize how important that promotion could be for me?"

"You obviously don't realize it will be important for me too," Kate said as kindly as possible, considering the fact that his inflexible attitude was swiftly pushing her to the limit of patience. "I'm very excited about the offer because, whether you know it or not, I want to advance in my career as much as you do in yours."

"Damn, I don't believe this," Joe muttered, pushing his fingers through his hair. "You mean to tell me that you're willing to leave Raleigh? And me, just for a better job?"

Kate's sigh was of the exasperated variety. "If I'd turned down the offer and you'd been given a chance at the promotion, you would have jumped at it, wouldn't you? You'd have left Raleigh and me, just for a better job? Right?"

"Sure, but that's not the same thing at all. I'm a . . ."

"Don't say it. The fact that you're a man doesn't make any difference," she cut his words off sharply, the delicate features of her face taut and unyielding. "If I had refused the promotion, and you had accepted it, everything would have worked out the same. Either way, one of us will be in Raleigh and the other in

Charlotte. Since the offer was made to me first, I'll just be the one in Charlotte."

Apparently realizing his caveman reaction was getting him nowhere fast, Joe tried to change tactics and gave her a too indulgent smile. "Come on, Kate honey, you can't really be serious about all this. You . . ."

"I suggest we talk about this later when you've decided to be reasonable. Right now I want to get back to work," she said, wasting no time getting up from the table. When Joe unexpectedly grabbed onto her suit jacket, she glared down at the hand clutching the cloth. She ground her teeth together. *"Do you mind?"*

"Hell, yes, I do mind," he muttered, his newfound charm flying right out the window. "Tell me, Kate, how did you get Cordell to give you the promotion? Did you do a lot of sweet talking that night he drove you home from the restaurant?"

The skin beneath the back of her collar was becoming increasingly hot. "I don't like your insinuation, Joe, not one bit. I didn't even know this position in Charlotte would be open, so how could I have sweet-talked my way into it?"

"All right, all right, maybe I was out of line accusing you of that," Joe admitted but not very graciously. Then he laughed but the laughter was a hollow unpleasant sound. "It's hard for me to believe, but you've proved Cordell right. He told me you'd accept the promotion, and I assured him you wouldn't. Boy, am I going to feel like a fool the next time I run into him."

"That makes two of us then because he told me you wouldn't like it if I accepted, and I assured him you'd be happy I'd been given such a great opportunity. Isn't it funny how wrong we both were?"

"Not particularly." Joe's grip on her jacket relaxed somewhat, and he shook his head perplexedly. "I still don't understand why you were offered the job."

"Because I have more retail experience," Kate answered softly, most of her irritation dissolving. She was genuinely fond of

Joe and didn't like to see him suffer disappointment even when that disappointment was unfounded. She touched light comforting fingertips to his cheek. "Nathan simply believes that more experience makes me better qualified."

"*Nathan*, is it?" Joe sneered, suspicion becoming a bright glitter in his eyes. "Maybe I could understand this whole situation better if you told me exactly what kind of relationship you and *Nathan* had in the good old days in Charlotte."

For an instant, she was sorely tempted to do just that, tell Joe the entire unvarnished truth about Nathan and the past. But to have done so would have been deliberately hurtful, and she bit the words back just in time. Instead, she gave Joe no answer at all and swept his hand away from her and left the breakroom.

Outside in the hallway, she stopped at the water cooler, her hand shaking as she raised the flimsy paper cup to her mouth. As she tossed the cup away in the trash can, she thought that if Nathan had actually tried to damage her relationship with Joe, he couldn't have done a more thorough job of it than he'd done today. It was at that moment the suspicion took root—maybe damaging that relationship had been Nathan's intention from the beginning. Maybe that was the only real reason he had offered her a better job.

For the remainder of the afternoon, Kate's unbidden suspicion festered until she couldn't banish the increasingly disturbing thought from her mind. Maybe Nathan got some sort of perverse pleasure out of ruining her relationship with other men. Maybe he was one of those men who might not want a woman for himself yet still didn't want her to be close to anyone else either. Maybe he simply liked to manipulate her life. Maybe . . . oh, maybe a million things, she thought at last with a frustrated curse beneath her breath. No longer able to bear the persistent suspicion, she decided to confront Nathan with it.

Unfortunately, she discovered that Nathan had left his office at three o'clock and wouldn't be returning until the next morning. That didn't stop Kate. With great discretion she managed to learn where Nathan was staying while in Raleigh. After nervously picking at her steak and salad dinner in her apartment, she drove to his hotel. He was in, but the desk clerk had to call his suite to announce Kate, and to her eternal chagrin, he obviously hesitated before granting her permission to visit him. The clerk gave her a look of insolent amusement, and embarrassment and irritation tinted her cheeks pink, but despite the mortification she felt she took an elevator up.

Kate's heels sank down into the thick plush carpeting in the corridor as she knocked lightly on Nathan's door, which he opened almost immediately. With a gesture he invited her in, and as she walked past him, she tried not to notice how disturbingly attractive he was in navy pants and a cream rugby-style shirt. Dressed much more casually than he always was at the office, he reminded her more of the Nathan she had known too well six years ago, and at the moment she didn't need to be plagued by memories like that.

Since she had entered the sitting room of his suite, he hadn't spoken, and by the time she settled herself on the rose damask sofa, she realized he intended to wait for her to say something. She did and minced no words as she went about it.

"I want you to tell me the truth," she announced bluntly, gathering all her intrinsic courage around her like an invisible shield. "Why are you really offering *me* this promotion?"

With a puzzled quirk of one eyebrow, he sat down beside her. "What kind of question is that?"

"A serious one, so please tell me the truth. Did you give me the promotion because you think I deserve it? Or did you do it just to hurt my relationship with Joe?"

"Is that what's happened? Is Joe angry because you've accepted a position he thinks should have been offered to him?"

"Let's just say he's upset."

"Ah, I see. I can't say I'm very surprised," Nathan said casually, draping a long arm over the back of the sofa. "Katie, some men simply can't deal with women more successful than they

61

are, and I have to admit I suspected Joe might be that type of man."

"And . . ."

"And from what you say, he's proven he is."

"Oh, for heaven's sake, Nathan, stop dodging the real question!" Kate exclaimed, not bothering to hide her exasperation. She was in no mood to allow him to play a cat-and-mouse game, and there was defiance in her eyes as they held his. "Did you promote me because I'm the best person for the job, or because you were pretty certain Joe would react badly to the news?"

"That's a ridiculous question, Katie. I told you this afternoon that I never play around when it comes to business," Nathan stated flatly, a flicker of irritation passing over his face and indicating he resented her suspicions. "For the last time, I'm telling you I offered you the position in the home office because you're qualified to fill it. If Joe happened to react childishly, that's not my problem. It's his. And yours, I guess."

Instinct told Kate she could believe him, and suddenly she wished very much that she hadn't come. Nathan was right. She did know him well enough to realize that he was too shrewd a businessman to manipulate his employees merely for his own personal amusement. Berating herself for letting Joe's juvenile behavior arouse such silly suspicions, she gave Nathan a brief nod as she slipped the strap of her purse up over one shoulder.

"You're right. The problem's Joe's. And mine," she said, her tone subdued. "It was unprofessional for me to come here and question your motives but . . . I just felt I had to make sure you were promoting me for all the right reasons. I'm sorry I bothered you. I'll leave now."

A hand came out to push back gently against her shoulder as she started to stand. Her gaze darted to Nathan and he smiled lazily. "Why go? Stay and we'll have a drink to celebrate this step upward in your career. Unless of course, you're afraid to be in my hotel suite alone with me?"

"White wine, please," Kate said crisply, laying her purse beside her as she sat back on the sofa. He had issued a challenge her pride forced her to meet because she simply couldn't allow him to believe she feared him. Yet, she experienced an uneasy flutter in the pit of her stomach while watching him cross the room to a small built-in mahogany bar. Why did he still look so good to her after all these years? Why couldn't she be immune to that aura of virile masculinity that clung to him like a second skin? Why couldn't she simply think of him as her employer because, after all, that's all he was to her now? But he was a man too, the only man she had ever known intimately. She had shared a night of ecstasy with him and that memory still had the power to take her breath away.

A dreamy luminosity softened Kate's eyes to lambent green as they slowly drifted over Nathan, who was walking behind the bar. He bent down to take a bottle of chilled white wine from a small refrigerator, and with that movement, the muscles of his broad shoulders rippled beneath the knit cotton of his shirt. An abrupt intense need filled Kate, a need to see him once again without a shirt. She remembered that not an ounce of superfluous flesh covered his large frame. She remembered the smooth texture of his sun-browned skin. She remembered . . . Shaking her head as if to reassemble her thoughts, she called herself a damned fool for falling victim to such erotic fantasies. Dragging her gaze from Nathan, she instead inspected the room. Obviously this was one of the most impressive suites in what was the finest hotel in Raleigh, and she admired the decorator's taste. Muted rose and gold and ivory were the colors predominant in this room, and she wondered if that color scheme had also been carried into the bedroom.

"Why don't you ask him to take you in there and show you? Why not just invite yourself into his bed?" she muttered with self-disdain beneath her breath. She really had to take herself in hand and stop this fanciful nonsense that was whirling through her brain. Nathan was dangerous enough without her succumbing to the sensuous side of her nature.

As Nathan returned from the bar to hand her a wineglass with the most fragile stem she had ever seen, Kate ignored the involuntary physical response she felt when his fingertips briefly brushed her own. Raising the glass, she took a sip of the sparkling wine, savoring it for a moment before swallowing it.

"Umm, that's delicious," she murmured with a wry smile. "Which probably means it would be beyond my price range."

Nathan smiled back rather absently as he once again sat down beside her. "Obviously Joe gave you a hard time this afternoon," he stated bluntly, dark aqua eyes seeking and holding hers. "I'm sorry he had to react that way."

Kate took a weary-sounding breath. "I saw a side of him today I'd never seen before, and he made some remarks I'd much rather he'd left unsaid." She fell silent temporarily, realizing she hadn't liked Joe very much this afternoon and obviously the feeling of disrespect had been mutual. He hadn't really liked her either because she had proven to be more career-oriented than he thought a woman should be. "He actually seemed to think I should refuse the promotion so it would be offered to him. I was astounded that he didn't realize that my work is important to me."

"As I said, I'm not really surprised he reacted that way," Nathan responded softly, watching her face. "Though I can't really comprehend an attitude like that."

"I know you can't," Kate murmured then suddenly decided she must be crazy to be confiding in Nathan, of all people. Yet, she knew why she did it—he was a tolerant man and always had been. He judged all people by character, and he judged his employees by that same criteria plus their abilities. She liked him for being that way. She could respect him, which made the lack of respect she was still feeling for Joe considerably more disturbing.

"Ah, well, I suppose Joe will get over being miffed," she said almost inaudibly, and she didn't sound particularly convinced. A rather sad little smile came to her lips. "You know, Nathan, whenever you and I are in the same place, we seem to make a habit of upsetting the life of some young man. We're really good at that, aren't we?"

"God, Katie, aren't you ever going to let go of that self-imposed guilt?" he muttered, taking her glass from her hand and putting it on a side table with his when her chin wobbled slightly. One arm went round her shoulders and a gentle hand guided her head to rest in the hollow of his shoulder. He silently stroked her hair, seeking to give comfort and succeeding.

Kate drew a long shuddery breath and relaxed against him, allowing her tension to flow out of her slowly. Nathan was strong, and right now she desperately needed his strength. She wanted a surcease from the haunting guilt she had borne in her soul for the past six years. Nathan could give her that because he didn't think either of them should feel guilty, and for this brief moment of time, she was going to allow herself to believe him. Even though he was wrong, even though she didn't deserve a second of peace, she felt she would go mad if she didn't get Phillip off her bruised conscience at least momentarily. She snuggled closer to Nathan, letting her arms go round his waist as she was filled with the keen longing that he could always drive her guilt away. Not that he would care to—his feelings for her didn't run that deep. But tonight she wasn't going to let even that matter. She needed his strength too badly, and she would take the brief but blessed peace of mind he could provide. Later would be soon enough to suffer with her conscience again.

Kate tilted her head back slightly to give Nathan a tremulous but grateful smile. "Thank you," she whispered. "I . . ."

"Katie, *Katie,*" he muttered, his deep voice husky as he swiftly lowered his head.

"*No!* Nathan, please don't! Just hold me, that's all I want," she gasped, but her plea was too late. And when his firm lips took possession of hers, her response belied her last words. Emotional need was heightened to a fever pitch as her physical desire at being close to him exploded in a flash of white heat within her.

Her arms tightened around him, and she went eagerly as he moved her onto his lap and removed her jacket while his mouth devoured hers with an ever-increasing slightly twisting pressure that quite literally stilled her breath. And she kissed him back, her soft warm lips parting, closing, caressing his. The muscles of the arms around her tautened. Imprisoning her in the circle of his powerful embrace, he crushed her to him, and she was a willing captive to the hands that cupped the sides of her breasts. The heels of his palms pressed into firm yet yielding feminine flesh. Kate moved sensuously against him, controlled by that inborn provocative instinct women possess. The reality of his superior strength, his clean male scent, and the hard lean feel of his body were becoming all that mattered now, and her own hands sought his hair, his neck, his shoulders, as if she couldn't get her fill of touching him. And she couldn't; she had to go on touching him especially as the kisses they exchanged became less urgent yet deepened to a slow, deliberate, mutual arousing of their senses.

The tip of his tongue opened her mouth wider. He tasted the sweetness within, causing molten fire to course through her veins. The sizzling heat was all-consuming, and her entire body was burning as dizzying desire sapped the strength from her limbs.

Nathan's hands roamed over every graceful curve of her slender body, tormenting her with the growing need to know a more thorough, intimate exploration. His touch was as light on her as hers was on him, but while her caresses were more tentative, his were expertly teasing and seductive. And she wanted to be seduced.

"Oh, Nathan," she breathed against the lips that nibbled the soft shape of her own. "Touch me."

"Yes, Katie, yes," he whispered, trailing searing kisses over the curve of her neck.

Kate's eyes fluttered open, and she became lost in the smoldering passion glowing in the depths of his. Her breathing began to quicken when his fingers moved to deftly unfasten the buttons of her blouse then slip that garment off her completely. He sought the hook of her bra, and even as he peeled the lace cups away, he lowered her down onto her back on the sofa. The bra joined the blouse on the floor. His hands played over her, fingers feathering her incurving waist and probing every inch of rounded slopes of strainingly taut mounds of flesh. His burning gaze held her spellbound, and when she began to make soft little sounds with every stroking caress, a slight smile tipped up the corners of his hard mouth.

Kate slipped her hands beneath his shirt, and she helped him off with it to seek the sight and feel of bare sun-bronzed skin. Her nails caught in the fine dark hair on his chest as she traced his muscular contours with her fingertips. A groan came from deep within Nathan's throat. Reveling in her ability to arouse him, she brushed the back of one hand across his flat abdomen just above the waistband of his pants. Muscles fluttered beneath her touch, and Nathan muttered her name hoarsely while entangling his fingers in her hair. He leaned over her to touch his lips to her own then lowered his head, and as his mouth closed with gently pulling pressure over the roseate tip of one breast, she cried out softly with the exquisite sensations that plunged with a keen rush through her and danced like wildfire over every inch of her skin.

His hands spanned her waist as he searched for the zipper of her skirt. He slowly and deliberately moved it down its tracks and gently pulled the material past her hips to lie in a heap at her feet. His fingers moved in slow tortuous circles over the delicate structure of her lower back, following the insweeping arch that curved downward and outward into the gentle swell of her hips. Kate was trembling now, feeling more vibrantly alive than she had in six years. Her caresses were no longer tentative. She became bolder, running her fingertips down his lean sides to graze them teasingly over sensitive skin just beneath the waistband.

"*Katie*, you've always known how to drive me crazy," he

whispered unevenly into the deep-scented valley between her breasts. "I want you so badly."

And she wanted him, so much that she could hardly stand it when his fingers slipped between hers, and he raised her hands above her head, denying her the pleasure of touching him. Even teeth nibbled the hardened nubs of first one breast then the other; his tongue explored the hot skin of her nipples, making her nearly wild with desire. Through half-closed eyes, she gazed down at his dark head. Remembering all he had once meant to her, she knew instantly that he still was and always would be everything to her. She loved him still; she had never stopped, and her heart was certain of that fact now. Compared with her love for him, her feelings for Joe paled to insignificance. Only with Nathan did she feel complete, and when he released her hands, they cupped his face, urging his mouth up to hers again.

Plundering lips ravished the softness of her as the control Nathan had exercised over his own desire ceased to exist. He moved above her, the weight of his long lithe body pressing her down into the sofa cushions. She wrapped her arms around him and her cushioned breasts yielded beneath his chest. His potent lingering kisses drew from deep inner recesses all the love she had kept hidden even from herself, filling her with bittersweetness. He lifted his head, and she gazed up at him until he eased off her lacy panties and the thick fringe of her lashes dropped down to veil the adoration and desire she knew must be mirrored in her eyes. A raging battle commenced in her. She ached to surrender completely yet was in an agony of fear. Giving her love to Nathan likely meant he would tear her emotions into shreds again, but at that moment she couldn't deny him. She pressed one shapely thigh between the hard strength of his, felt the powerful upsurge of his response, and was lost in it.

"Sweet Katie," he said and groaned. "Let me love you."

"Oh, yes, Nathan, love me now," she breathed, pain intermingling with her need to give, as she knew he meant love in the physical sense while she meant far more than that. But a woman's love, too long denied, eventually has to find release, and even when it's not returned, has to be properly given. Kate was ready to give and tried to blink back the tears of conflict that sprang to her eyes. A few tears escaped to trickle downward, and as Nathan trailed a strand of feather-light kisses across her cheeks, he tasted the saltiness of damp skin.

"God, Katie, don't do this to me now," he muttered roughly, brushing away a fat teardrop with the edge of his thumb as he leaned on his elbows over her. And seeing the moisture that glistened in her eyes, he clenched his jaw tight and lifted himself up to sit on the edge of the sofa beside her. "Get dressed," he commanded harshly. "I've never resorted to taking a weeping woman to bed, and I'm not about to start now."

She touched his back. "But Nathan, I . . ."

"Go home. Snuggle up with your precious guilt. I won't take anything from you that you don't want to give."

She did want to give yet didn't, terrified of the devastating loneliness she knew would come when it all ended between them again. If only he loved her too . . . but he didn't, and she averted her eyes from him as she sat up to put her clothes back on with shaking hands.

Nathan had gotten up to stride over to the bar where he stood, his back to her. Smoothing her tousled her hair, she swept up her purse and moved toward the door, stopping before she opened it. She looked at him, her heart aching with a need to go and run her hands over the straight implacable line of his bare back. Yet that would have begun the insanity all over again, and since there was nothing at all she could say to lessen the angry disdain he was obviously feeling for her, she left him. With him she left a great deal of herself, but he didn't know that. And had he known, she was sure he wouldn't have cared.

CHAPTER FOUR

Kate shifted in her chair as she waited for Nathan to look up from his desk. Although the papers he was scanning appeared to be quarterly sales reports, and important business, he had called her into his office five minutes ago and, except for acknowledging her presence, hadn't spoken to her since. Deciding she might as well while away the time by looking out the window, she gazed at the swaying branches of trees in a city park, a cool green oasis amidst rising buildings. Her thoughts drifted so much so that Nathan had to say her name to reclaim her attention.

"Sorry to keep you waiting, but I wanted to look through this report today," he said as she turned her head to look at him with an uncertain smile. "Now we can get to the reason I wanted to see you."

"Molly said it was important but she didn't know why."

Nathan nodded. "It is important, and what I have to say may cause you inconvenience, but that can't be helped. I realize it was only a week ago that I offered you the position in the home office, and this is very short notice, but you're going to have to be in Charlotte this Monday. When Betty heard we had a replacement for her, she decided to use accrued vacation days to fill out the time until her official retirement date. And that means we'll need you Monday."

"But it's already Thursday, and I know I can't get moved out of my apartment here by this weekend," Kate explained, spreading her hands in a resigned gesture. "Luckily, I have found a young couple to sublet the place, but I still don't have an apartment to go to in Charlotte. If you could just give me another week, I . . ." Her words trailed to a halt as he slowly shook his head. "But Nathan . . ."

"Sorry, Katie, but the personnel department in the home office is a big operation, and Gary needs an assistant to keep it running smoothly. What I suggest is that you come back to Raleigh next weekend and arrange the move and until you find an apartment in Charlotte, we'll provide accommodations. Now that makes it somewhat less inconvenient, doesn't it?"

Kate was able to agree to some extent. "Well, it sounds as if everything is going to be pretty hectic and rushed for a while, but I'm sure I can handle it."

"I know you can, just as I know you can be ready to drive with me to Ten Oaks tomorrow evening for the weekend," Nathan said flatly, his gaze steady on her. "Another suggestion: Pack everything you'll need next week in Charlotte. Save us a trip back here Sunday."

"You never once mentioned that I would have to go to Ten Oaks this weekend," Kate uttered weakly, her eyes wide and tinged with a hint of apprehension, some of the color gone from her face. "Why . . . should I have to go there? I . . . don't understand."

"It's very simple. You've never met Gary Roberts, and since the two of you will be working very closely together starting Monday, I decided this weekend at Ten Oaks would give you a chance to get acquainted. I'd like you to be ready to leave by six tomorrow evening."

Kate slowly shook her head, appalled that he would even

suggest taking her back to Ten Oaks with him, back to where Phillip had died. He knew very well how overwrought emotionally she had become the last time she had visited. "I can't go there, Nathan," she said, her voice rasping. "You must know I just can't make myself go back."

He quirked one eyebrow. "Oh, but I'm afraid I have to insist this time, Katie."

"I won't go," she shot back with a stubborn uptilting of her chin. "I don't see that it's at all necessary for me to go, and I just won't do it. With Evelyn so close by, I . . ."

"Katie, *enough* of this nonsense," Nathan commanded, getting up to come swiftly around his desk. He towered over her, aqua eyes glinting as he stared down at her uplifted face. "You've run away from Ten Oaks *and* Evelyn far too long already. It's time to go back now and face your unreasonable fear of her and the place. And you're going back *with me* tomorrow night."

Kate twisted her hands in her lap, and there was supplication in her eyes as she returned his piercing gaze. "Nathan, you . . ."

"This is something you'll have to do, Katie, whether you want to or not. It's not all that unusual for me to have members of the home office staff up to Ten Oaks on weekends where we can combine relaxation with business. In your new position, you'll simply have to become accustomed to going there on occasion. If you can't do that . . ."

Although he didn't complete what he had started to say, the unspoken threat was not lost on Kate. If she couldn't become accustomed to occasional visits to Ten Oaks, she would be promptly demoted and sent back to Raleigh in all probability. Pain, overriden by a surge of resentment, tightened her features. "You can be a callous, almost cruel, man sometimes, Nathan," she accused tersely. "You really don't want to try to understand my feelings about Ten Oaks and Evelyn and . . . Phillip."

"Oh, I do understand," he countered, taking her chin between thumb and forefinger while looking deeply into her eyes. "But you've let those feelings torture you much too long. I intend to put an end to that."

"I wish you could," she admitted huskily even as she shook her head. "But I can never forget."

"I don't expect you to forget. But you can't do penance for the rest of your life for a tragic event that was never your fault in the first place. Come now, Katie, surely you're not too weak to face Ten Oaks and even Evelyn, if necessary?" Releasing her chin, he brushed back the sides of his tan coat and placed large hands on lean hips. "Of course, if you're certain you can't face going back there, I suppose you can stay here in Raleigh, and I can offer Joe the job."

He was practically blackmailing her! She wanted that promotion badly and he knew it. Yet it wasn't really her desire to advance her career that made her stiffen her spine and resolve firmly that she *would* go with him this weekend. Instead, she knew she had to go because he had cut too close to the bone with his roundabout challenge to prove to him that she wasn't a weakling. Deep in her heart she was secretly afraid that a weakling was exactly what she was. For six years she had been terrified at the mere thought of ever seeing Evelyn again or the place where Phillip had died. Now, for the sake of her self-respect, she knew she had to prove to Nathan and, more importantly, to herself that she was strong enough to face a past which needed to be reckoned with, even if that reckoning was very unpleasant.

Still looking up at Nathan, she at last breathed a long heavy sigh. "All right," she said softly. "I'll go with you since you aren't giving me much choice."

"I'm not giving you any. As your boss, that's my prerogative," he said, his expression unreadable. He returned behind the desk and sat down again. "Will you be needing part of tomorrow off to get together enough things to last you through next week? If so, you can have tomorrow afternoon."

"Thank you but that won't be necessary. I'll have time to get everything I'll need together tonight." Realizing she was being dismissed, Kate stood, then suddenly clapped light fingertips against her forehead. "Oh, I nearly forgot. There's something I hope you'll be willing to take care of after I've gone to Charlotte." As briefly as possible, she explained about the employees who had been temporarily laid off two weeks earlier. "I was told they would be rehired, so I practically promised them they would be, especially Mary Weaver. Her little boy's been very ill, and she's going to need a regular salary to help pay the medical expenses. Really, Nathan, all of these people were good employees and deserve to be rehired, and I'd feel much better about leaving if I knew you were going to take care of that."

"You really get involved, don't you?" he murmured, unfathomable eyes sweeping over her before he picked up a gold pen. "Give me their names, and I'll talk to Tilford and Joe about them either today or tomorrow, and tell them they're all to be called in to work again within the next couple of weeks."

After reciting the names and watching Nathan write them down, Kate hesitated, wearing a tiny questioning frown. "Maybe I misunderstood, but just then, you almost sounded like you aren't going to be here after tomorrow?"

"That's right. I won't. It's time to get back to Charlotte."

"But you said when you arrived that you might stay as long as two months!"

"So I did but in the two weeks I've been here, I've changed my mind. There's no basic reorganization needed in this store. Tilford's an excellent manager and there's absolutely no need for me to stay here any longer." Clasping his hands behind his head, he leaned back in his chair. "What's the matter, Katie? Is my return to Charlotte going to create some kind of problem for you?"

"No. No problem," she lied with as much aplomb as she could muster. "I was just curious, that's all. Well, better get back to my office. See you later, Nathan."

"Definitely," he drawled as she walked away toward the door. Kate shot a quick speculative glance back at him then went out with the growing suspicion there had been a subtle taunting note in his reply. Perhaps she wasn't quite as convincing a liar as she had imagined. But then, Nathan's revelation had taken her completely by surprise. She had expected him to remain in Raleigh for several more weeks, thus giving her the opportunity to become accustomed to Charlotte before he returned to the home office. Now she knew different. From the very beginning, she was going to have to cope with a new home, new job responsibilities, and coworkers, *and* Nathan too. *What fun.* Nathan would have been more than enough to deal with all by himself.

Back in her office, Kate spent the next two hours busily trying to tie up loose ends. She jotted down notes in personnel files, wrote a couple of memos to Joe, one of them telling him that she had spoken to Nathan about the rehiring of the laid-off employees, and generally took care of all the unfinished business she possibly could. While she was initialing the May sales report from the Miss Sophisticate department, her door opened and Joe came in.

Looking up, Kate smiled. She was really surprised Joe had sought her out. He had been sulking all week, speaking to her only when necessary, and he had even made a lame excuse to cancel their regular as clockwork Wednesday night date. He had come to see her now, though, so perhaps he had realized he was acting like a sullen little boy and wanted to make amends. Kate was ready to forgive and forget.

"Hi, Joe," she said, a teasing sparkle in her eyes. "Goofing off again, I see."

Joe didn't smile back. Shoulders hunched, hands balled into fists in his pockets, he approached her. "I just heard on the grapevine that tomorrow will be your last day here," he announced, his voice pitch higher than she had ever heard it. "Is that just another rumor or is it the truth, Kate?"

"It's true." Tossing her pencil down onto her desk, she got up. "I'm needed in Charlotte by Monday, which is much sooner than I expected. Actually I have to leave Raleigh tomorrow evening. Nath . . . Mr. Cordell wants me to meet my new immediate superior this weekend, so we can start getting acquainted."

The entire time she spoke, Joe shook his head. Now he twisted his lips and made a sound reminiscent of a disbelieving snort. "You really amaze me, you know that? I can't believe you're going through with this. All week I've been expecting to hear you'd told Cordell you'd changed your mind, that you didn't want the job in Charlotte."

"But I told you I do want it. Very much," Kate replied, determined not to let him irritate her. She gave him a rather wistful smile. "I know you wish I didn't but I still do."

"Even though you know how upset I am about the whole mess?" Joe asked with a brooding scowl. "Or haven't you even bothered to notice I am upset?"

"I noticed." *How could I have missed?* she added to herself but continued to hold a tight grip on her patience. "But I think it's unreasonable of you to think you could make me change my mind about the Charlotte position by pouting and refusing to talk to me all week. Those kind of tactics don't usually work very well, Joe, and they didn't work with me."

"What the hell else was I supposed to do? It didn't do me any good to try to talk you out of this silliness," he muttered, swiping a lock of hair back off his forehead. "If you go to Charlotte, and I guess you're really going to, what's going to happen to us, Kate? Tell me that."

"The same thing that would have happened if you were going there, and I was staying here, I guess. It's no different this way around, Joe. We won't be seeing each other every day, but there'll be weekends."

"Yeah, I guess so," he mumbled while reaching out to pull her to him. Holding her in his arms, he looked down at her as she gently patted his cheek, as if he were a child she was consoling. He frowned. "You do care about me, don't you, Kate?"

"I care," she answered. And it was true. She simply didn't care the way he expected her to, especially knowing now how he had expected her to sacrifice her career for him. The way he had treated her, his anger and hostility, made her realize that she could never love him, never feel for him what she felt for Nathan. He could never be more now than just a friend.

At six fifteen Friday evening, Nathan and Kate left for Ten Oaks in his Jaguar. They took interstate highways and two hours later had passed through Winston-Salem. The mountains lay ahead, and Kate's stomach muscles began to tighten. Thus far, the ride had been enjoyable. The Jaguar was luxuriously comfortable, and as usual, Nathan proved a very interesting conversationalist. Yet, now renewed dread was gnawing at Kate, and she talked less and less with every mile that passed. Near Wilkesboro, Nathan left the interstate and turned onto a narrow, secondary road, which became increasingly winding in its steeper ascent. Small farms, some of which were evergreen nurseries that help provide the nation with live Christmas trees, were patchwork shapes along the landscape. Cows grazed in lush rolling meadows, and the fragrances of laurel, flame azalea, and purple rhododendron scented the cool early night air. Dusk was dropping a secret veil on the rising peaks of the Blue Ridge Mountains, casting them in soft purple shadow. Kate took a deep but silent breath as she gazed up into the hills. In a way, she was happy to be here. She had always loved the pristine beauty of the region, and now to a certain extent she felt she was coming home again. Yet, near the edge of conscious thought, as usual, was the uncertainty, the fear that returning to these lovely virginal mountains would surely reopen wounds that had never completely healed.

Despite the growing darkness, the Jaguar's headlights illuminated landmarks that Kate recognized. They registered on her mind with rushes of memory until she sat very still gazing out her window as she watched for them. Lost in thought, she reacted slowly when Nathan swung the car right at fork in the road. She glanced forward, then swiftly squeezed shut her eyes,

77

but, unfortunately, not before she saw in the headlights' beam the scarred trunk of the huge ancient oak that split the road.

She groaned softly and didn't resist when Nathan slowed the car and his hand on the nape of her neck urged her to him. She buried her face against his arm and cried almost silently, whisper quiet sobs shaking her body. He stroked her hair.

"I know how you must feel," he murmured, stirring a tendril of hair with his breath. "I always try to avoid looking at that tree myself. But it's never easy for anyone to have to see the place where a friend has been killed. My parents are going to see if they can get the state to cut that tree down. Before Phillip's accident and since, several other people have hit it. The fork in the road takes them by surprise, I guess."

"It couldn't have surprised Phillip," Kate mumbled. "He certainly knew the fork was there."

"He'd been drinking and he was speeding. He lost control of the car."

"I know you like to believe that."

"I believe it because that's undoubtedly how the crash happened," Nathan said, his tone low pitched and sincere. "Katie, Phillip wasn't a stupid young man. If he had been suicidal that night, he wouldn't have crashed his car to kill himself. That would have been too risky. Instead of dying instantly, he might have suffered a great deal and ended up maimed for life. Phillip would never have taken that chance. That fact alone makes me know that the crash was an accident."

Katie couldn't argue because what he had just said did make sense. Yet she was filled with too many doubts and self-recriminations to be completely convinced. She accepted the white handkerchief Nathan handed her and wiped away the tears from her cheeks without speaking. Slipping out from beneath the arm that lay across her shoulders, she put some distance between Nathan and herself again and stared straight ahead as they drove through a forest of evergreens whose branches met above the road to form a tunnel of greenery. Out of the corner of her eye a few minutes later, Katie caught a glimmer of light to her right, but she didn't dare look directly at Evelyn's house as they drove past it for fear of crying again. At the moment, she wasn't prepared to look at the house Phillip had grown up in; seeing the crash site had in itself been traumatic enough for one night. Instead, she escaped the niggling pulls at her conscience by concentrating exclusively on the road that meandered along before them. She was watching for the familiar entrance to the Cordell property, and after Nathan had driven on little more than a mile, the beam of the headlight reflected on the white stone pillars of the gate that interrupted a long stretch of split-log fencing. Another, different emotion tugged at her heart. She would be seeing again for the first time in six years the house where she had spent that night with Nathan and willingly given a love she now knew had been very real indeed.

The gate between the stone pillars was open as always, issuing its own welcome as Nathan drove through, down a paved lane that bisected a fenced-in pasture where sleek Thoroughbred horses grazed in the daytime. What had once been the secluded estate of a wealthy tobacco scion from the Piedmont was now a country retreat for the Cordell family. When in residence there, the family blended into community life rather than placing themselves above their neighbors. For that reason, people in the county tended to forget the family owned a chain of elegant department stores that stretched over the entire southeast. Every Cordell seemed like one of them and was liked and respected by everyone, except of course, Evelyn Hughes.

Despite the unconscious downcurve of her lips, Kate managed to thrust all thoughts of Evelyn to the back of her mind. Sitting up straighter in the passenger seat, her breathing accelerating slightly, she saw patches of light between swaying branches of the cedars and pines that formed a semicircle around the back and sides of the Cordell house. Nathan made another turn, and they drove beneath the gnarled limbs of the double lines of oak trees that bordered the drive, five on each side. The graystone house rose up to greet them, friendly light spilling out of every multipaned downstairs window. Kate's gaze roamed slowly over the elegantly simple structure and beyond to the lush rolling sweep of the lawn in front of it. A sudden joy, as if she had at last found home again after long years of wandering, surged in her heart, although she knew she had no right to feel that way at all. Ten Oaks was not her home. It never had been and never would be where she belonged. The house drew her and she was eager yet dreaded to go inside.

After Nathan killed the engine and got out of the Jaguar, Kate followed, shouldering her own tote bag when he removed their other luggage from the trunk. A suitcase in each hand, he escorted her across the low-slung veranda supported by white stone columns. They had nearly reached the front door when it abruptly swung open from inside and Callie Dobbs, the Ten Oaks' housekeeper, squinted out into the glare of the veranda's wall mounted lights.

" 'Bout time you got here. You said it'd be nine thirty or thereabouts, but I'll have you know it's after ten o'clock. You know how I fret when you're late coming, Nathan," she fussed half-heartedly, relief in her pleasantly lined face even as she perched her hands on ample hips and assumed a scolding posture. Then chastisement was forgotten as she reached up and patted Nathan's lean cheek, as if he were her own son. Clucking insistently, she took one of the suitcases from Nathan despite his protest, said a curt hello to Kate, and marched briskly ahead of Kate and Nathan across the wide foyer. Light caught in the prisms of the crystal chandelier overhead and danced in reflections scattered over a space of the gleaming hardwood floor. A tightening ache gathered in Kate's throat at Callie's cold greeting and as she looked all around, she was assailed by converging memories. Moving like an automaton, she kept pace with Nathan as he followed Callie up the winding stairs. At the top of the steps a wide hallway stretched out toward both sides of the house, and when Callie turned right, Kate swallowed convulsively. Nathan's bedroom was in this wing of the house; she certainly remembered that, and if Callie intended giving her a room in the east wing too, it really wasn't such a wise idea. Yet, she could hardly protest when the housekeeper stopped at a door only two away from Nathan's room. To have insisted she be moved farther away from him would have been far too revealing not to mention terribly ungracious behavior from a houseguest. With a wan smile in answer to Nathan's parting comment that he would see her downstairs in a few minutes, Kate followed Callie into the first bedroom while he continued down the hall to his own.

Decorated with early American antiques with a patchwork quilt spread on the bed and brightly colored hooked rugs on the hardwood floors, Kate's room was as warm and welcoming as the house itself had always been. Unfortunately, Callie's attitude no longer corresponded with the cosy surroundings. A distinct iciness appeared in the housekeeper after she placed the suitcase on the cedar chest between two windows then turned to stare suspiciously at Kate. Then, ignoring the younger woman's hopeful smile, she marched purposely out of the room.

Once Callie had been very fond of Kate, but that was obviously no longer true. Judging by that withering stare, she apparently believed Kate had quite some gall even to show her face here, considering the disaster she had caused during her last visit. And although Kate was admittedly disappointed in the housekeeper's less than friendly treatment, she understood it. After all, she hadn't been exactly eager to return to Ten Oaks. Nathan had coerced her into doing it.

Knowing Nathan was never blamed for anything in Callie's estimation, Kate allowed her shoulders to droop the tiniest bit before squaring them again. Grim determination tightened her jaw as she began methodically unpacking her luggage. Since she was only going to be at Ten Oaks two days, she could surely endure even Callie's disapproving glances for that long.

After Kate's belongings were all put away in the proper places, she went into the bath that adjoined her bedroom to quickly run a comb through her hair, which was fairly windswept after riding several hours with the Jaguar's windows down. It had been worth a few tangles, however, to be able to breathe in fresh clean country air, and she really couldn't care much that some of the curl had gone out of her tresses. While trying to smooth away a stubborn wrinkle from her navy linen skirt, she left her room to run lightly down the stairs. She paused in the foyer a moment, heard voices in the kitchen at the back of the house, and went to join Nathan there.

As Kate pushed open the swinging door and entered, Nathan looked up at her. With a wry smile, he swept a hand over the abundance of food laid out on the wooden table before him. "Hope you're hungry. As usual, Callie's prepared enough to feed an army."

Callie, turning away from the refrigerator with a pitcher of iced tea, shook her head in protest. "You used to be able to eat more than that by yourself."

"I used to be a growing sixteen year old but I'm quite a bit older now," he retorted with a grin. "That's a fact you like to forget, Callie."

"That fried chicken looks delicious," Kate remarked, smiling at the affectionate bickering while she sat down across the table from Nathan. "And you've made some of those delicious cucumber sandwiches, Callie. Those always were my favorite."

The pitcher of tea was put down with a little bang on the table. The housekeeper's nose wrinkled slightly, and there was no voiced response to Kate's complimentary comment. When Callie abruptly walked away toward the sink, Kate pretended not to notice Nathan's questioning frown.

"I hope Gary Roberts is planning to join us in this feast," she said instead while pouring tea into Nathan's glass, then her own. "I think the three of us can do justice to all this tempting food. Don't you?"

"I'm sure we could *if* Gary were here. But he's not arriving until tomorrow," Nathan said dryly, his gaze holding hers. "Didn't I mention that?"

"No. You didn't." Lowering the thick fringe of her lashes to conceal the uneasiness she knew must be stealing into her eyes, Kate carefully selected a golden brown chicken leg as she added, "Then with your parents in Europe, the two of us will be alone tonight? Right?"

"Not precisely. Callie and Fred are always here."

Looking quickly back up at him, Kate lowered her voice to a near whisper. "But they still live in the garden cottage, don't they? Or have they moved into rooms here in the house?"

"No, they're still in the cottage," he whispered back with a careless shrug. Sardonic amusement produced a half smile. "But you needn't worry about being in the house alone with me, Kate. As I told you the other night, I don't take weeping women to bed, so all you have to do is shed a few tears to protect yourself from me."

A faint blush rose up Kate's neck to bloom enchantingly pink in her cheeks. She glanced back over her shoulder, and as she had suspected, Callie had one ear cocked toward the table as if she were straining to hear every word they uttered. The housekeeper felt she was part of the Cordell family thus their business was her business. But it wasn't her natural curiosity that disturbed Kate, it was Nathan's inconsistent attitude that bothered her. At times he could exhibit a seemingly genuine understanding of her feelings. Then he could turn right around and become taunting and cavalier, as if he enjoyed making her uncomfortable with his outrageous and mocking comments. Knowing she would be wise to start expecting the unexpected from him, she arranged her face in composed lines, gallantly pretending his last remark hadn't unnerved her in the slightest.

"You really shouldn't say such things in front of Callie," she murmured at last rather primly. "You've probably embarrassed her."

"Don't be prudish, Katie. Callie isn't embarrassed and she

83

certainly wasn't born yesterday. She knows we were lovers once, and she probably thinks we are again or will be soon."

"You'd better set her straight then because she's certainly mistaken. That part of our relationship ended long ago and will never be repeated."

"Never say never, Katie," he advised softly, the teasing expression on his lean face evolving into one that was far more disturbingly solemn. His eyes narrowed and darkened and seemed to search the secret depths of her own. "It isn't wise to make promises to yourself that you might not be able to keep later on."

Refusing to be baited into continuing a battle of words neither of them were going to win, Kate simply lifted her gently arched brows at him before taking a bite of Callie's county-reknown chicken. Despite her misgivings at being at Ten Oaks again, Kate's appetite was good. In addition to the chicken she ate two of the small cucumber sandwiches and ended the repast with a fresh locally grown peach. Nathan, too, obviously enjoyed Callie's impromptu but more than ample late evening meal, and when they were both finished, Kate offered to help the housekeeper tidy the kitchen.

"No, thank you, miss," was Callie's quick reply, her cold tone at variance with her warm mountain drawl. "I can get it done faster by myself."

Weariness exaggerated the hurt Kate felt because of Callie's deliberate unfriendliness. For a second she caught her lower lip between her teeth then gave Nathan a forced and unconvincing smile. "Well, then, if you'll excuse me, I am pretty tired. I think I'll go up to my room now."

He simply nodded, saying nothing as she left the kitchen, but she only got as far as the top of the stairs before she heard his quiet cat like tread, turned, and found he had caught up with her. With the touch of a large hand on her shoulder, she stopped in the upstairs hallway to look up at him.

"Don't mind Callie," he said. "She doesn't really mean anything by the way she's acting. She's just being a little stand-offish."

"More than a little and the reason for the way she's acting is very clear. She used to be very fond of me but not anymore."

"She's just very protective. You know she considers herself and Fred as part of the Cordell family."

"You mean she feels she has to protect the family from *me*?" Kate asked, laughing and shaking her head. "What a crazy notion. I certainly can't understand where she got an idea like that."

"No, I'm sure you can't. There always was a great deal you didn't understand. Maybe you were just too young or maybe you didn't want . . ." Nathan's enigmatic statement trailed off into an expectant silence in which the very air around them seemed suddenly charged with tension. In one stride, he eliminated the distance between them.

Kate's heart began a violent triphammer beat that was nearly dizzying in its rapidity. A change had come over Nathan, and he was no longer either teasing and taunting or gentle and under-standing. Now he merely seemed dangerous, yet the danger she sensed was so oddly hypnotic that she had to make herself step back from him only to realize she was trapped against the corri-dor wall. The touch of Nathan's hands as they possessively spanned her waist was electric, and her breath was released in a soft involuntary gasp as shockwaves of physical response rip-pled over her from head to toe. The flat surface of the wall felt cool against her overheated flesh even through the fabric of her blouse until Nathan lifted her chin slightly with one lean finger and bent down to touch his lips to the frantically pounding pulse in her throat. All semblance of coolness vanished, and every inch of her skin burned hot with the caress. The protests she needed to utter found no voice, and she could only move her head slowly from side to side in denial until he stilled that movement by cupping her chin in one hand. His other hand roamed over her, following her gracefully sweeping curves. Firm warm lips moved upward to nibble with seductive gentleness on the softer shape of hers. Kate's legs went weak with warmth beneath her weight, and if his supporting arm hadn't drawn her tight against him, her knees might have buckled. Her fingers clutched his shirt front, partly pressing against him in resistance, partly stroking over him in surrender. She felt his lips form a slight smile on her own.

"It's been so long since you've been up here with me," he whispered, the tip of his tongue opening her mouth a little so that his breath feathered the veined inner flesh of her cheeks. When she trembled, he kissed her, firm lips lingering. "My room hasn't changed since the last time, Katie, and you liked it then so come spend tonight there with me."

He was testing her. She was suddenly sure of it, and because she was far too aware of how easily it would be to fail his test, she was filled with resentment. She loved him yet he cared so little for her that he could play these tormenting games with her emotions without a twinge of his conscience. Perhaps it was time to give him back some of his own medicine, she decided, though not very wisely. Responding on impulse and a need for some revenge, she stretched up on tiptoe and wrapped her arms around his neck. She moved provocatively, pressing the length of her slender but more than adequately curved body against the hard long line of his. Promising kisses she trailed along his strong jaw. Then she kissed each corner of his mouth and sighed with eager acquiescence as his hand on her rounded hips arched her against the hard power of aroused masculinity when he widened his stance. What had begun as an avenging ploy became a danger she recognized all too clearly. Her pretended response was verging close on the edge of reality. Because she loved Nathan, she ached to be near him, and it was only strength of will that enabled her to chant repeatedly to herself, "This is only an act; you won't give in to him; this is only an act."

Her common sense screamed at her to retreat now while retreat was still a possibility, but she ignored it, too intent on carrying her avenging game to the end. Her soft lips clung to

Nathan's, and she begged him breathlessly to kiss her again and again.

Only when his heart was pounding steadily at a fast pace against her breasts did she lean back in his arms to gaze drowsily up at him. "Oh, Nathan, I shouldn't go to your room," she whispered tremulously. "I want to but . . . I shouldn't."

His answer was a swift and strong repossession of her mouth, and this time Kate drew away not to tease but to gain control again of her spiraling senses. The desire for revenge was swiftly taking second place to stronger sexual desires. Needs only Nathan could satisfy threatened to overcome her original intent. But Kate was strong. She fought the physical ache that had begun to rage inside her, and the stronger and more potentially devastating emotional needs if for no other reason but to keep her self-respect. On her very first night back at Ten Oaks she couldn't possibly allow Nathan to take her to his bed. Her pride would never stand for that. Steeling herself against the arousing effects of his caressing lips and hands, she disentangled her fingers from the vibrant thickness of his hair. Shaking her head she pulled back, putting a distance of inches between them. "I can't, Nathan," she murmured, her head down. Strangely enough, she was unable to look at him, although this was her small moment of triumph. "I just can't."

A finger beneath her chin tilted her face up, and to her astonishment something akin to amusement mingled with the glint of passion in Nathan's aqua eyes. An almost indulgent smile touched his carved mouth. "You were taking quite a chance, Katie," he said softly. "What if I had believed you were serious and expected you to finish what you'd started? You *were* very convincing, but I'm going to let you get by with that, this one time anyhow. I guess it was just your way of getting back at me for making you come here." He actually laughed, though not unkindly, at her wide-eyed look of total surprise. Then he released her and turned toward his own room.

Watching him walk away, Kate felt more than a little ridiculous, but at least she was always courageous enough to admit it when she was wrong. She took a hesitant step after Nathan and quietly called, "I owe you an apology." She met his gaze directly when he stopped to turn back toward her. "I . . . What I just did was childish."

"Yes, a little. But it was also amazingly innocent," he answered, his eyes drifting over her in disruptive appraisal before he gave her another, too knowing, smile. "I'm beginning to suspect I'm the only lover you've ever had. Is that true, Katie?"

That was something she *was* unwilling to admit to him. She simply stared at him and offered no answer at all to his question, relieved when his smile faded to nonexistence.

"We'll talk about this again tomorrow," he promised then opened his door and disappeared into his room.

Kate slipped into her own room, closed the door, and leaned back against it with a confused sigh. She had certainly botched that one. Shaking her head bewilderedly, she wondered why she could never emerge victorious in an encounter with Nathan. In the end he seemed to always come out the winner. Perhaps that was because she was in love with him, but his deeper emotions were not involved at all. He wasn't vulnerable while she was and that obviously made all the difference.

After a warm bath, Kate got into bed and switched off the lamp on the table beside her. She was sleepy, but after spending such a nerve-wracking evening, she rather doubted she would rest peacefully during the next several hours. She was right. She dreamed about Nathan all night.

Gary Roberts didn't arrive at Ten Oaks on Saturday either. It seemed he had come down with some sort of virus. And Kate had no choice except to believe that was the truth since she answered the telephone herself when Gary's wife called to give his apologies. She sought out Nathan in the stables and delivered Gary's message.

Hooking his thumbs in belt loops of faded denim jeans, he

nodded. "Hope it's nothing more than one of those twenty-four-hour bugs. Something like this can't be helped, of course, but I did want you and Gary to have some time to get acquainted before Monday."

"So did I," Kate told him, leaning over the side of a stall to pat the rump of a magnificent black stallion. She glanced back over her shoulder at Nathan. "Since Gary can't make it, though, maybe we should just drive on to Charlotte."

Nathan matter-of-factly shook his head. "No. I see no point in doing that. Gary's sick so you won't be able to see him in Charlotte either. We'll just stay here and relax."

Though Kate doubted she would ever be able to truly relax at Ten Oaks again, she didn't voice that opinion, and as it turned out, the day she and Nathan spent was very enjoyable and mercifully devoid of tension. In the stables she was fortunate enough to witness the gangling first steps of a newborn foal that had been sired by a onetime Preakness winner. After Nathan managed to pull her away from that adorable creature, the two of them walked leisurely through the peach orchards that marched in neat rows of trees south of the house. Later, after an early dinner that freed Callie and Fred for a visit with their daughter in Jefferson, Nathan suggested he and Katie go riding. It was the perfect evening for it. Twilight was still perhaps two hours away and the air was cool and deliciously refreshing. A pleasurable excitement rose in Kate while she saddled a roan mare, and Nathan saddled the black stallion she had earlier admired.

They led the horses out into the stableyard where they mounted them. Turning toward the northeast in the direction of Evelyn Hughes' small farm, Nathan tugged gently on the reins.

Kate tensed. "I'd rather . . . Couldn't we ride in some other direction?" she called after Nathan. "Any other direction?"

Half turning in the saddle, he looked back, darkening eyes burning into hers. "We never rode this way with Phillip. That's why I thought you might prefer it. But if you're that afraid of seeing Evelyn, which is highly unlikely, we'll . . ."

Pushing her unreasonable fear aside, Kate shook her head emphatically. "No. You're absolutely right. Let's go on this way." Touching her heels against the mare's sides, she rode up alongside Nathan, relieved when he initiated a leisurely conversation as if he had already forgotten her compulsive protest about the direction they were taking. White fluffs of cumulus clouds glided against the backdrop of darkening blue sky, drifting so low at times it seemed they would catch and drape like chiffon stoles around the tips of the shadowing mountains. Soon Kate was immersed in the mystical serenity of the surroundings. She felt a delicious sense of peace and freedom as she appreciatively inhaled the faint fragrance of wildflowers that wafted through the air. Held to a slow walking gait, the horses followed an old tractor trace that was slowly being narrowed by encroaching natural vegetation.

Pristine silence enfolded Nathan and Kate, causing them to respectfully lower their voices whenever they spoke to each other, which became less and less frequently. No words were needed. Togetherness came in the sharing of nature's exquisite loveliness, and some time later, when Kate gently reined in the mare and dismounted, Nathan watched while she stooped to pick a flower at the edge of the tractor trace.

"Blue-eyed grass," she whispered, holding up a slender blade topped by a tiny starlike blue flower for him to see. "I haven't seen one of these in years. Isn't it beautiful?"

With the tip of one long tanned finger, Nathan touched the fragile blossom and nodded. "Would you like to pick some to take back to your room?"

She smiled wistfully. "I'd better wait until I can bring damp paper towels to wrap the stems in, or they'll wilt before I can get back with them. Maybe tomorrow I can come out here and get some then."

With lithe athletic ease, Nathan swung down from his saddle and took the mare's reins and the stallion's in one hand as he and Kate continued on foot. After several minutes, a lush green meadow rolled in gentle hills before them. A rock-strewn bubbling stream frolicked, clear waters molten gold in the sunset's glow until it wound downward and disappeared around a bend in a stand of majestic cedars. A steeper hill rose in the distance, crowned with a strand of wire fence that stood sentinel between Ten Oaks and Evelyn Hughes's property. Kate stared sadly at it for a brief moment then turned her eyes elsewhere. Even the symbolic animosity conveyed by that metal barrier didn't appreciably diminish the greatest inner peace she had felt in six years. Perhaps the mountains had curative power because the agony of regret she lived with constantly was certainly eased here. She was comforted by the timeless continuity of the ancient surrounding hills, which had been there eons before her and would still be there eons after she was gone. The place she had known and loved would endure and that in itself gave her a very real sense of peace.

Caught up in the magical wonder only the purity of nature can bestow, Kate slipped her fingers between Nathan's when he took her hand and led her toward a lone pine that stood halfway down the first rolling hill of the meadow. She leaned back against the rough trunk while he looped the reins of both horses around a sturdy branch of a nearby elder sapling. Given slack, they began to graze contentedly.

Joining Kate, Nathan leaned on one hand against the tree trunk and followed Kate's gaze as she looked dreamily out over the green carpeted meadow. A cathedral-like stillness enveloped them, and as if drawn by some irresistible force, both their heads turned at the same moment. They looked at each other for a long time, their silence breathtaking and spellbinding.

At last Nathan moved. One hand curved the back of Kate's slender neck. "Your eyes have lost that shadow of sadness," he murmured huskily, leaning closer. "You look as happy as the Katie I once knew."

Soundlessly, she moved into his arms, feeling that was where she belonged. She *was* happy. For that precious moment in time, she *was* the Katie he had once known, loving and unafraid to give her love completely. Her lips parted at the first touch of his, and as he gathered her to him, she wrapped her arms tightly around his waist, yielding effortlessly when he lowered her to the soft grass at the base of the tree. Her legs entangled with the long length of his as his weight pressed her slight frame down against the soft turf. Warmly alive and responsive, she felt as if she were melting into him as she returned his kisses with an expertise he had taught her long ago. The curve of her lips teased the firmer shape of his, and she gloried in the invading exploration of his tongue slipping evocatively into her mouth. Joyous inevitability bloomed fully in her chest and her hands swept eagerly over his strong broad back, pressing him down invitingly against her. Warm and utterly pliant, she became irrevocably lost in the increasing demand of his roving caresses, and she arched upward, evoking a tortured groan and the unrestrained male response she had been seeking. Loving him without inhibition, wanting only to give everything of herself now, she guided a lean, sun-browned hand upward to cover one full, cushioned breast. Strong yet incredibly gentle fingers pressed into her rounded softness, sending a keen piercing thrill rushing through her. Weakness dragged at her lower limbs, and she ached for his lovemaking, wanting that more than she had ever wanted anything in her life.

Stroking the muscular contours of Nathan's taut shoulders, she breathlessly sought his lips while he undid the top three buttons of her blue oxford shirt. A fingertip trailed lazily downward into the hollow between her breasts, and her need to give her love to him and take whatever he could give became a driving force that banished all reasonable thought. Whispering his name, she dropped a hand down to the buckle of his belt then moaned softly when her fingers were caught tightly in his and immediately stilled.

"Don't stop," she breathed against his ear. "Nathan, love me now."

"No, not yet. Not here," he muttered roughly, gazing down at her, passion glimmering in his eyes. "I hear thunder in the distance. And, more importantly, I want all night in my bed with you. Do you want that too?"

"Yes, oh, yes," she answered, lost in the possessive glow of his gaze as he raised himself up and drew her swiftly up beside him. His arm remained around her waist while he untied the horses, and suddenly without warning he swept her up to put her on the stallion's saddle.

She looked down at him in surprise. "But the mare. How will she . . ."

"She'll follow us. You're riding with me," Nathan explained, swinging up onto the saddle behind her. "I want to hold on to you because I won't let you change your mind this time."

As his hand glided across her abdomen, drawing her back against him, she relaxed and shook her head. "I won't change my mind, Nathan," she promised. "I think it's too late."

"I know it is," he murmured, his lips descending rousingly on hers when she tilted her head back to look up at him. And the kiss that lingered and deepened as they rode toward Ten Oaks only hinted at the passion to come.

CHAPTER FIVE

The horses had been stabled and provided with a treat of an apple each to accompany their dinner of grain and hay. Hand in hand, Nathan and Kate walked to the house. In the lighted foyer, he shut the door firmly behind them, closing them in together and closing the rest of the world out. Kate stood watching him, waiting, and when he turned to her again, his narrowed gaze wandering hungrily over her, she held out a hand. He took it, pulled her slowly into a possessive embrace, and kissed her with such increasingly persuasive power that her desire rose in tumultuous spirals to match his own. His arm firmly around her, holding her close to his side, they went up the stairs and down the dimly lighted hallway to his bedroom.

The lingering illuminating remnants of the sun just dropping down behind the peaks of the mountains bathed the room in lambent gold, outlining in shimmering gilt the wide high carved bed and the matching mahogany dresser, bureau, and small round table. Kate stepped inside, feeling almost as if she had suddenly gone backward six years in time. Nathan was right. Very little, except the draperies and counterpane, had changed since she had last been here, and, with a brief closing of her eyes, she saw mentally the girl who had stood in this room then. She was no longer that girl, so timid and uncertain. Now she was a woman, and it felt right to be with Nathan in his room again. Some perfectly natural shyness lingered deep within her—it *had*, after all, been six years since the last time—yet shyness was overshadowed by her womanly need for the man she loved more than anyone else in her life.

As Kate stood in the center of the room, Nathan went past her to draw the drapes open. The sun's afterglow spilled in on them, silhouetting him in the frame of the window and casting her in pale bronze where she stood, as if transfixed, looking at him.

Nathan smiled gently and moved one beckoning finger. "*Katie,*" he whispered, his low coaxing tone sending shivers of sensuous excitement up and down her spine. "Come here."

She went. And he moved toward her. They met at the foot of the bed. Taking her face between his hands, he bent to trail kisses along her eyebrows, over the lids that fluttered shut with her soft sigh, and beneath high contouring cheekbones into the slight hollows of creamy smooth skin. Kate turned her head a fraction, her soft lips seeking the enticing firmness of his, and a muffled sound of pleasure and pure joy escaped her when his mouth claimed her own with hardening, heady demand. Fully aware of barely leashed passion raging within him, Kate still moved nearer, helpless to prevent herself from brushing her lissomely curved body against the unyielding length of his. Nathan's response was dizzyingly swift. Urgent hands spanned her waist, fingers spreading open over gently rounded buttocks. The aggressor, he arched her to him, bending her back slightly over a supporting arm as he tasted the honeyed sweetness of her parted lips, tantalizing with the feathering strokes of his. They kissed again and again, but soon even those most intense and passionate kisses were not enough for either of them. Nathan slipped a hand beneath Kate's blouse, the ball of his thumb tracing small circles over her bare midriff until muscles were fluttering beneath the caress. Gazing down at her through half-closed eyes ablaze with desire, he drew her hands together over the center of his chest, guiding small fingers to the buttons of his shirt.

"Undo them," he coaxed hoarsely. "Now."

Kate unfastened the buttons with a provocative slowness that seemed to heighten Nathan's desire to a fever pitch. His aroused masculinity pulsated with demanding power against her flat abdomen. Her ability to evoke such overwhelming passion made a secret bewitching smile touch her lips as she gazed up at him through the thick fringe of half-lowered lashes. Lazily, she opened the tan western shirt with brown cording, her fingertips grazing over the muscular contours of his bronzed chest, her palms lightly playing over fine dark hair. At last she pushed the shirt off his broad shoulders, pulling it off to let it slip through her fingers to the floor behind him. On tiptoe, she moved her lips over the skin stretched taut over his breastbone and rubbed the tip of her tongue against him.

Nathan's hands spanning her waist tightened with undeniable demand. "Enchantress. Two can play this game," he whispered, his low rough tone issuing an exhilarating warning, his evocative smile promising delight. He proceeded to remove her blouse, more swiftly than she had taken his shirt off, but her bra came off with such deliberately tantalizing slowness that Kate had to bite back a plea for him to accomplish the task. He slipped the straps from her shoulders then looked long at the rise and fall of her scantily covered breasts. Straining at the pinnacle of white lace cups, the sensitive tips were visible, and he probed them with stroking fingertips. The delicate wisps of fabric did nothing to buffer the electric shock of his touch. Kate's eyes fluttered shut. She gave a low moan as nipples hardened to sensitized nubs, which Nathan gently squeezed between thumbs and forefingers. Then even he could no longer bear to prolong the seduction. Deftly, he unhooked the back closure of the bra and removed it. It drifted from his fingers to fall with a lacy whisper onto the chest at the foot of his bed. His eyes glinted while he played his hands over upsweeping mounds of feminine flesh then he lowered his dark head and his lips followed the fiery path his fingers had blazed. He kissed every inch of the sloping curves of her breasts then closed his mouth with moist pulling pressure around first one caramel peak then the other.

From that moment Kate was lost completely. He controlled her now, and she adored what he was doing. Between his tongue and the roof of his mouth, the tender flesh of the tips of her breasts tingled with wild sensations that radiated in rushing ripples downward and outward, filling her with needs she had no hope of denying. Hooking her fingers around belt loops of his jeans, she clung to him, her breath coming in soft little gasps while his mouth continued to possess her full throbbing breasts.

By then Nathan's breathing was labored too, and there could be no turning back. He lifted his head only to lower a hand to the snap at the waistband of her jeans. He opened it, lowered the zipper, and brushed the denim fabric down over her hips. His palms skimmed the sensitized skin of the backs of her thighs and calves as he pushed the jeans down around her ankles. He straightened, watching as she gracefully stepped out of them and her shoes at the same time. Hard warm hands feathered down her shapely arms then he hooked his thumbs beneath the waistband of her panties and went down on his knees before her as he slowly drew them down her legs. Those he removed himself, gripping her waist to balance her as he lifted one slender foot then the other. He stood again to hold her slightly from him, his eyes devouring the in and outsweeping curves of her nakedness.

"God, you are exquisite," he groaned, reaching for her hands and bringing them to the buckle of his belt.

Kate undid it but her fingers were trembling so violently—not with fear but with heightening anticipation—that he completed the task for her with an endearingly indulgent smile. Unclothed too, he shuddered slightly when she ran her hands slowly up and down his lean hard sides. Even the sun's afterglow had faded now. Deepening darkness was shadowing them. Nathan reached around Kate to switch on a bedside lamp that filled the room with soft light.

"I want to see you," he murmured, a muscle ticking in his tight strong jaw as his gaze roved with burning intensity over her. He touched her face, her hair, the sloping curves of her breasts. He stepped closer. "You are so lovely, Katie."

"You're lovely too," she breathed, half giddy with the emotions aroused by the sight of his lean virile body. It was almost as if she were seeing him this way for the first time. For too many years, she had erased from her mind the memory of how he had looked that night. But now she was remembering. Everything. All the delight she had experienced then she ached to experience again. She wanted to give all her love to Nathan and to share ecstasy with him. Tonight she wanted no one else in the world to exist except the two of them, and for once she was glad Nathan had the power to banish everything from her mind except love and need.

In the pale light, Kate's skin glimmered opalescently, and Nathan seemed unable to tear his gaze from the fascinating shimmer. "Your skin's like satin," he said, his tone hushed. "I could look at you forever."

"Touch too," she invited, moving closer, hands covering his to guide them along her in-sweeping waist. "I want you to touch too." Perhaps it was the relaxing day they had spent, and the mystical magic of their twilight ride that allowed her to respond so uninhibitedly. Or perhaps it was the years she had suppressed her own sexuality that now caused that very human drive to blaze like an out of control wildfire through her veins. Or perhaps it was simply that a girl's adoration which had never really died had risen out of the ashes of hurt and disillusionment to become the strong enduring love of a woman. Mainly, it was that. Kate's love conquered inhibitions and reawakened a sexuality she had desperately kept hidden even from herself. Emotions unchained now, she couldn't turn back the tide of her feelings. Nor did she want to. Nathan brought her fully alive, and she had to touch him with love and be touched by him. Her hands cupped the strong column of his neck. Her smile was soft as she looked up at him. "Kiss me. Hold me," she said and sighed. "Let me touch you."

"God, I want you to," he growled, clasping her small wrists to pull her hands downward across his chest to the taut flatness of his abdomen. With a deep throated groan, he took her into his arms so swiftly and tightly that she was lifted up against him. Only the tips of her toes brushed the hooked rug beneath his feet. His mouth covered hers and her arms wrapped around his neck as she pressed nearer to him. The cushioned softness of her breasts were crushed against his muscular chest and fine dark hair tickled her skin. Fingertips probed the delicately structured flesh and bone of her back until she was quivering.

Nathan made a low triumphant sound and reached down to throw back the covers on his bed. In one fluid motion, he swept her up and laid her down on smooth sheets that were cool to her overheated skin. He stood looking at her, and she was unable to prevent herself from looking at him, taking in the copper glow of his skin, the broad strength of his shoulders and chest and lean tightness of his tapered waist. His legs were long and strong, muscular but not sinewy, and when he widened his stance to lean over her, braced by his extended arms, she reached up to run her fingertips over the finely carved planes of his face.

He smiled at her, and if it couldn't be love that gentled the glint in his aqua eyes, it was something so akin to deep affection that Kate could lose herself in hopeful pretense. She smiled back, her heart feeling as if it might burst with love for him. "Come to bed, Nathan," she whispered tremulously. "Come to bed now."

He lowered himself down onto his side next to her, a firm forceful hand on her waist turning her to him. Her arms slipped around his neck and their eyes met, creating for her a breathtaking wonder that ran like quicksilver through her. Though she couldn't breathe, she was unable to break that spellbinding visual contact, and soon she felt she was drowning in mysterious dark blue depths. Her own green eyes were luminously soft, the dark pupils wide and brimming over with love for him. Although she knew he could hardly fail to recognize the intensity of her feelings, she didn't really care if he did realize how she felt. She simply couldn't get enough of looking at him, and when he moved his head toward her, his dark face filled her vision, driving the last shreds of rational thought from her brain.

Nathan's initial kisses were unhurried, cajoling, as if he meant to still any lingering uncertainty she might have. Such easy unrushed seduction merely served to intensify her love for him and further inflame her senses. His every touch became like lightening bolts flaring through her, igniting every nerve ending until each caress was ecstasy yet also an agony that only total fulfillment could transform to utter delight. Knowing this, Kate ached for the moment of complete union, but Nathan made her wait, thereby transporting her into a realm where she began to tremble with each kiss and caress, enslaved by the keen, nearly maddening power of her own response.

Kate wanted him so badly. Her own hands flowed over him, adoring the smooth taut texture of his skin, cherishing the long masculine line from shoulder to muscular calf, loving the minty taste of chiseled lips and warm mouth. Her need of him was so intense that expertise was born of necessity. She discovered places to touch that made his breathing faster and more shallow, and her fingertips played around and inside the curve of his ears then trailed down to brush the taut, flat nipples encircled by dark hair. Her own lips became irresistably provocative, catching at the fuller lower curve of his. Her small even teeth nipped teasingly and soon, very soon, he responded with all the impassioned virility she had wanted. With a groan, Nathan covered her hipbone with one hand, impelling her flat back onto the bed, one long hair-roughened leg pinning both hers as his upper body covered hers. His hands swept into her hair. He held her head fast. His mouth descended, taking her lips with an insistence that tolerated no denial.

After a glorious eternity, he released her to look down into her face. "Not yet, Katie," he muttered. "Not yet."

His lips and tongue repossessed the swollen tips of her breasts, pulling gently at the sweet flesh, sending shattering currents of wild desire plummeting through her. Pleasantly rough fingertips rubbed back and forth across her bare abdomen, and Kate moved, unable to lie still, her hands skimming feverishly over his back.

At long last, he slipped a hand between shapely thighs, his thumb brushing upward over her exquisitely sensitive flesh, and as Kate gasped softly with pleasure, he drew one small hand downward.

"Touch me," he commanded huskily, and when she did, self-control evaporated in the hot flaring of his response. His eyes pierced the dreamy depths of hers. "Oh, God, I've dreamed about you touching me like this . . ."

"Oh, Nathan. . . ." she breathed, her heart thudding as he slowly moved between her long elegant legs. His mouth touched hers. Her lips clung to his. A hand slipped beneath her, cupping her rounded hips, lifting them upward to receive him. His throbbing hardness glided into her feminine warmth.

Kate's nails pressed into the corded muscles of Nathan's shoulders, and she breathed a long shuddering sigh of joyous delight. Her arms wrapped around his waist and words of love nearly tumbled from her mouth. She didn't—couldn't—utter them, fearing he might feel compelled to say he loved her too. All she said was, "Nathan, oh, Nathan," while with her soul and with her body she gave all her love to him.

"Sweet Katie. I was the only one. Wasn't I?" he whispered, burying his face in the scented thickness of her hair.

With the intuitive knowledge that Kate was inexperienced except for that one night spent with him, Nathan reintroduced her to lovemaking with endearing tenderness. He was in no way an impatient and inconsiderate lover. He was demanding yes, even forceful, but his insistence was a compelling proof of his passion that was undeniably arousing. His desire heightened Kate's; hers heightened his, on and on in an endless spiraling of keener and keener sensations until they reached a plateau where their joining became less feverish and more a lasting sharing exploration Kate wanted never to end. They seemed to merge into a single being, hearts beating together as one and time was suspended as they were swept away in a physical and emotional wonderland of delights. Her pleasure pleased him; his pleased her and slowly but inexorably this blissful plateau, rapturous as it was, became the prelude to ultimate fulfillment. Together they were rising, rising in a whirlwind of enchantment, and Kate was wildly alive with the deepening ripples of ecstasy Nathan now seemed to fully control. He was holding his own need strictly in check as he bore her up swiftly to the finely honed edge of sharply penetrating delight. She was suspended there for an exquisite instant before he took her over the edge and wave after wave pulsated within her, radiating from the centermost core of her being. Kate cried out his name softly, and the cry mingled with his low triumphant groan but even as the waves were receding for her, leaving in their wake a delicious contentment, he unexpectedly bore her up once more to that piercing pinnacle. Crashing waves undulated through her this time, and Kate felt faint. She bit down hard on the side of her left forefinger to keep from crying out Nathan's name too loudly, and as she drifted down into the warmth of supreme satisfaction, she burrowed her hot face into the hollow of his shoulder, her heart brimming over with her love for him.

Kate kissed the strong tendons in his brown neck and the firm line of his jaw. Her hands grazed over his smooth naked back and downward to cover lean taut hips, silently urging him to assuage his own seemingly intolerable need. She arched upward, straining against him, breaking the tight rein he had held on his passion, and she was filled with an indescribable happiness when hard marauding lips plundered the softness of hers. Yet he seemed reluctant to burden her with his full weight until she wrapped herself closer and pressed him down invitingly. Then he was no longer capable of gentleness. Her slight body yielded acquiescently beneath him. He began to move more swiftly, taking her with all his superior strength and such a compelling urgency that she gloried in the giving.

Afterward they lay wrapped in each other's arms, their breathing slowing as they exchanged lazy contented kisses. Nathan smiled and touched Kate's tousled hair. She hesitantly looked up at him, unsure of saying what was so closely guarded in her heart. She smoothed his brow with her slender fingertips. "I want you to know, Nathan," she began tremulously, "you have been the only one in all this time."

Nathan lowered his head. "Sweet Katie . . ." he whispered against her mouth, brushing her lips gently. "I thought so . . . and I'm glad. But you know that wouldn't have made any difference to me, because what we shared tonight was right, Katie," he murmured sleepily. "It always is, isn't it?"

"Yes," she confessed because it was true. It had been right, and she was so very glad she had allowed herself to belong completely to him again. Even if she never received his love in return, she couldn't regret giving him the gift of her love, which always had been and probably always would be exclusively his.

Callie and Fred had Sundays off, and early in the morning Kate helped Nathan with some necessary chores in the stables. Their work was nearly completed when she impulsively decided that she did indeed want to return to the tractor trace for a small bouquet of the star-tipped blue-eyes grass. After saddling the roan mare and bringing damp paper towels in a small plastic bag from the house, Kate settled onto the saddle and smiled down at Nathan as he promised to follow her immediately after administering medicine to an ailing stallion. Then with a click of her tongue and a gentle bounce of her heels against the mare's sides, she rode away from the stables toward the northeast.

The clear mountain morning washed the rolling hills with pale gold sunshine. With her deep breath of the fresh clean air, Kate closed her eyes briefly and smiled to herself. Alone for these several minutes until Nathan rode out to join her, she could truly savor memories of the night they had shared without fearing he would detect in her expression the depth of her feelings for him. Alone, she could sigh softly as she recalled both his passion and his tenderness and the intimate camaraderie that had been between them since they had gotten up practically at dawn's first light. Though Nathan was an habitual early riser, Kate was more inclined to linger cozily beneath the covers as long as possible, and although she had awakened to his playful kisses, he had finally had to resort to lightly tickling her feet to get her out of bed. That lighthearted beginning of the day lingered with her now as she urged the mare into a smooth gallop along the winding trace. Exhilarated by the swift fluid motion of the horse and the cool wind lifting her hair from her nape, Kate bypassed the blue-eyes grass to continue the ride on to the meadow.

In the paler light of early day, the frolicking stream was a silver ribbon festooning the lush green grass, and the slight glare on the water made Kate squint and look away toward the pine tree beneath which she and Nathan had stood last night. Now two chipmunks played among the thick roots until the sound of hooves thudding on the springy turf caused them to scamper quickly away. As they vanished around the tree trunk, Kate smiled indulgently then glanced up without thought toward the peak of the hill rising before her. Her breath caught in a gasp as she saw the solitary figure standing on the Cordell side of the wire boundary fence, and she reined in the mare abruptly, knowing even from this distance that it was Evelyn Hughes, who stood still as a statue glaring down. Kate sat as if rooted in the saddle, surprised to find Evelyn on Cordell property, but as astonishment subsided, she urged the horse forward again, up the hill toward the fence. Her first inclination had been to turn and ride swiftly away but that would have been an act of cowardice. Besides, it was Phillip's mother who stood looking down at her, and deep inside Kate harbored the hope that perhaps if she spoke to Evelyn now, they could begin to put the painful past behind them. At the top of the rise when the ground leveled off again, Kate dismounted and led the mare behind her as she went to face Evelyn directly over the barbed-wire strands. While the older woman's sharp eyes raked over her from head to toe, and something very like loathing hardened what had once been an attractive face, Kate remained speechless, and the slim hope she had harbored for a reconciliation slowly died.

A deliberately malicious smile moved Evelyn's tightly pressed lips. "I saw Nathan Cordell kissing you in the meadow yesterday evening. I knew it was you! I knew it!" she spat out, her voice not particularly loud but shrill. It was almost as if daggers were shooting from her eyes as she sneered at the western shirt Kate was wearing. It was Nathan's and its great size covering her slight frame made Kate look provocatively sensuous. "*Look at you.* Nathan got a whole lot more than kisses from you, didn't he? I saw you riding back toward the house. *Both of you on his horse!* I knew what the two of you would be doing last night!" She stepped menacingly nearer the fence, hands balled into fists at her side. "You have some nerve coming back here and falling into Nathan Cordell's bed at the snap of his fingers! I can't believe you'd ever want to show your face around here again, after what you did to my Phillip!"

Having listened to the virulent tirade in silence, Kate shook her head sadly now. Surprisingly enough, no agonized feelings of shame swept through her; instead, she only felt an immense measure of pity for the bitter woman who confronted her with such hate and enmity. Although she realized nothing she could say would alter Evelyn's obsessive animosity, the affection she had once shared with the older woman prevented her from simply turning and leaving. Pity and decency kept her from taking that easy way out. Eyes darkening with compassion, she unconsciously half extended one hand.

"Evelyn, I'm sorry it's upset you so to know I'm here," she said quietly, sincerely. "When I came I hoped you wouldn't have to see me because I knew it would reopen old wounds if you did."

"You're shameless. Shameless!" Evelyn shot back. "You say you didn't want to hurt my feelings? Then why are you here?"

"Nathan is my employer now. The Cordell chain bought the Raleigh store I worked in," Kate explained gently. "I've been transferred to the main office in Charlotte, and we came to Ten Oaks this weekend on business. But the man I was supposed to meet here was . . ."

"I reckon you're going to try to tell me what you and Nathan Cordell did last night was work?" Evelyn interrupted cuttingly with a curl of her upper lip. "Well, I doubt that very much unless prostitution is your business now."

Rose color tinted Kate's cheeks as she breathed deeply. Even the accusations hurled at her lacked the power to shame or anger her. Still, all she could feel was pity. "Evelyn, this is all so useless," she murmured, wrapping the reins more tightly around her fingers. "I know all too well how very much you hate me. But what good does it do you or me to have this hatred between us?"

"It does me good, that's what! I wanted to tell you to your face what I think of you. You cheating little hussy, you killed my Phillip!"

Kate winced but shook her head. "No, Evelyn, I didn't kill Phillip," she replied, and at that moment an incredible serenity flowed through her because she knew what she had said was the truth. Six years ago, she had been irrationally emotional and unable to accept Nathan's reasonable explanation of Phillip's accident. But she was a woman now, older, wiser, and in the past few weeks she had obviously been far more receptive to Nathan's theory than she had realized until this very minute. Everything he had said now made perfect sense. She hadn't killed Phillip because Phillip hadn't killed himself. As Nathan said, Phillip was never stupid, and trying to commit suicide in a car crash would have been far too chancy for him to have risked it. Remembering now all the times she had chided him for driving too recklessly and too fast, she was able at long last to believe that what had happened to Phillip had been an accident, pure and simple. She still deeply mourned his death and felt some guilt for having been with Nathan when it happened. But the burden of responsibility she had imposed on herself—with Evelyn's inimitable help—was mercifully lifting, enabling her to deal more rationally with the woman's hate and vindictiveness. If she hadn't known she would be violently rebuffed, she would have touched Evelyn's cheek comfortingly. Because such a gesture couldn't be made, she held out both hands imploringly instead.

"I really can say now that I don't think I killed Phillip," she repeated gently, lifting a silencing hand when Evelyn opened her mouth to utter an undoubtedly caustic retort. "No, please just listen to me for a minute. I know you believe I killed Phillip or was directly responsible for his death. You've proven you believe that every year by sending me a card on his birthday. You wanted to cause me pain, and you certainly succeeded because I let you. But we've both been wrong all these years, Evelyn. Phillip didn't kill himself. He had an accident."

"No. Because you were cheating on him, he drove straight into that tree on purpose! I know that!"

"Do you? Or do you just need someone to blame for the terrible thing that happened? Deep down inside surely you know that with me or without me, Phillip would have wanted to go on living. He loved life."

Sudden confusion registered on Evelyn's face then vanished, and she shook her head emphatically. "Well, I still don't believe it was an accident but even if it might have been, you're still the blame. He wouldn't have been so upset and driving recklessly if you hadn't been cheating on him. You're to blame, no matter what you say."

Pressing her fingertips against her forehead, Kate released her breath in a deep sigh. "All right, Evelyn, all right. If it makes you feel better, I admit I was responsible for upsetting Phillip. But I didn't make him drink too much or drive too fast and too recklessly. And I wasn't cheating on him. I'd broken our engagement, even told him I was involved with someone else. I loved Nathan—I've discovered I still do—and I'm not going to apologize for loving him ever again, even to you because I'm not ashamed of how I feel."

"*Nathan Cordell,*" Evelyn spat out the name as if it were poison in her mouth. "You silly little fool, don't you know how many women have spent weekends with him here? How can you love a Cordell? You ought to know you can't trust a one of them."

"I only know that you've let your hatred for the Cordell family become all twisted up in your grief. And because I loved Nathan instead of Phillip, you've turned that hatred toward me too. Right now, what I regret more than anything else is what you've let all this do to you."

"Don't fret about my misery. You'd be better off to fret about how miserable you're going to be when Nathan is through with you. You're such a ninny." Evelyn twisted her lips derisively. "If Phillip had lived, I hope he'd have had the sense not to marry a woman like you. You don't even know that Nathan is using you. He wouldn't ever have married you six years ago. He would have married Lydia if the scandal about you and him hadn't embarrassed her so much. But she's divorced now and going around with Nathan again. He brings her here more than he brings anybody else. Bet you didn't know that. He's just using you again. Now you fret about that."

Kate could say nothing. She had wondered for weeks if Nathan was simply trying to use her, and in the back of her mind, there had always been that nagging thought that he was actually committed to Lydia. Doubts she couldn't banish. And it wasn't at all reassuring to have those doubts voiced as absolute facts by

Evelyn now. But Evelyn hated the Cordells; it wasn't wise to believe every nasty accusation she made about them. Yet . . . Kate groaned inwardly. She felt so confused. This emotional battle Evelyn was waging against her was beginning to fray her nerves. She couldn't take much more of it.

"Maybe I am being used," she conceded, her voice low, her tone subdued. "That's just a chance I'll have to take, I guess." She spread her hands resignedly, and there was much somberness in her face as she looked at Evelyn. "But I still worry about you. Hating me and every Cordell in the world won't ever bring Phillip back. I'd gladly have you hate me if it could but it can't. I know it's time for me to stop blaming myself for not being able to love Phillip. Don't you think it's time you stopped blaming yourself for being the one who told him I was with Nathan that night: I think it is. You weren't responsible for what happened either."

"I've never blamed myself! You did it! You . . . you *tramp*," Evelyn cried furiously, stepping forward, raising a hand palm outward and moving it swiftly in a direct line toward Kate's face.

A deep authoritative voice coming from halfway down the hill caused Evelyn to hesitate enough to lessen the impact of the swinging slap she delivered against Kate's left cheek. Even so, the slap did sting and left a faint red imprint of fingers on slightly paling skin. Kate hadn't attempted to ward off the blow and still stood unmoving as Nathan rode up, dismounted, and strode toward Evelyn.

"Go home," he told the older woman, pity tempering to some extent the anger that hardened his features when she snatched away the arm he had lightly grasped. He took it again, his grip firmer but still gentle, and purposely turned Evelyn around. "Go home. Cool off a little. I'm sure you've done enough damage for one day."

Evelyn balked, started to say something, thought better of it, and marched stiff-spined back across the field toward her own meadow. Nathan turned back to Kate, but she was already on the mare, her unusually pale face devoid of expression. Honoring her self-protective silence, he mounted the black stallion again and said nothing as they rode back to the house, rubbed down the horses, then turned them into the pasture to graze.

Still silent, Nathan followed Kate into the house and closed the front door behind them. In the foyer he reached toward her, but suddenly very close to tears she half-turned away. Too much had happened in too little space of time. Last night she had given wholly of herself to Nathan, and this morning she had been ripped to shreds by Evelyn. Her emotions were overwrought. Added to her sorrow for Phillip, pity for his mother, and her intense love for Nathan was the phantom of doubt Evelyn had succeeded in resurrecting in her mind. What *was* the relationship between Nathan and Lydia now? What if Evelyn hadn't been exaggerating? Was it possible that he was considering marrying his former fiancée? Kate couldn't bear to think of that now when only last night she had begun to feel the slightest hope that Nathan's feelings for *her* might eventually evolve into love. She just couldn't let go of even that slim hope so soon, especially when she had reason to suspect what Evelyn had claimed. Yet, the seed of doubt had been planted, and now she felt terribly confused. Head lowered, she didn't move when Nathan stepped up close behind her.

"Katie," he murmured. "I'm sorry that had to happen. It was just bad luck for you to run into Evelyn out there."

"It was bad luck for her to see us together in the meadow yesterday evening. She guessed that . . . we'd spend the night together," Katie replied almost inaudibly. "I think she was waiting for me today, hoping I'd come, so she could attack me again for 'killing Phillip.' "

"Which you're apparently beginning to realize you never did. I heard the last of what you said to Evelyn, that you think it's time to stop blaming yourself for what happened. All I can say is thank God. I was wondering if you were ever going to give up feeling guilty."

Kate gave a sad little smile. "Oh, I still feel a responsibility for Phillip's death," she admitted but failed to add she felt that because she had upset Phillip by breaking their engagement the day he died. "I guess I'll always feel responsible. I just felt forced to defend myself with Evelyn because she was saying the most awful things."

"But, Katie, for pity's sake, you can't go on blaming yourself forever," Nathan muttered, laying his hands on her slightly hunched shoulders. "Listen . . ."

"Nathan, please," she whispered, shrugging his hands away, suddenly finding his touch agonizing, not because of Phillip and the past but because of the uncertainty she was now feeling. If he was only using her . . . Everything was so bewildering and his hands on her only confused her further. She needed time to gather her thoughts into more rational order, and as he brushed the back of his hand across her cheek, she shied away.

Misunderstanding her reaction, Nathan jerked her around to face him. Fierce anger glowed in his eyes and strong fingers pressed downward to the delicate bones of her shoulders. "I've had enough of this nonsense, Katie," he growled. "You're not going to start that 'touch-me-not' act of yours again. I'm damned tired of having to fight your obsessive guilt. I guess Phillip was in the bed with us all last night, but by God, I promise you he won't be today!" With little gentleness, he swept her up into his arms and strode swiftly toward the staircase. Even her startled disbelieving gasp didn't deter him and his gaze caught and held hers, fiery passion combining with fury in the aqua depths of his eyes. His expression was stony, determined, and somehow almost savagely exciting as he lowered his head to whisper relentlessly, "This time, my sweet Katie, there'll be only two of us in that bed. I'm going to drive every thought of Phillip out of your mind. I'll make sure nothing exists for you except me and the pleasure we give each other."

Kate might have told him that he had done that very effectively last night, but she wasn't given the chance. Before she could utter a word, Nathan's lips were on hers, devouring sweet softness, claiming her very soul, and evoking such a rushing, uncontrollably passionate response that her mouth opened slightly but very invitingly beneath his. The light webbing of doubts that had clouded her thoughts were vanquished, at least temporarily, by the increasing power of a desire to surrender. Senses swirling, afloat in irresistable anticipation of dizzying delight, she slipped her arms closely around his neck as he quickly carried her upstairs to his room.

CHAPTER SIX

Nathan carried Kate to his window where he closed the drapes with an impatient jerk at the cord. Morning's brightest sunlight became a mellow golden glow as it filtered through the saffron fabric, and the bedroom took on a cool secluded look that was evocative in itself. Without a word, Nathan took Kate to his bed, putting her down amidst the tangled sheets then straightening to strip off his clothes.

Kate looked up at him, her heart and stomach muscles commencing to flutter simultaneously. She had never seen him like this, emotions erupting with such violence. What seemed a devastating anger was evidenced in the tightly strained line of his jaw, and as he stripped naked, she recognized fully for the first time the raw power contained in that lean muscular body. The age-old feminine fear of a male's superior strength surfaced from the deepest recesses of her consciousness, and suddenly she was scared of him, scared of the merciless blue gleam in his eyes. None of the familiar tenderness seemed to be left in him, and it looked to her as if he could hurt her and enjoy doing it. A half sob caught in her throat at the thought. If he used her brutally, she knew he would leave emotional scars that would never fade no matter how much time went by. Loving him as much as she did, she realized what kind of pain he could possibly inflict, and abruptly, the pragmatic Kate she had been for the past six years called urgently at her to jump out of bed, to run fast and hard, and to escape his wrath any way she could.

With the speed of a gazelle, Kate tried to scramble off the far side of the bed then cried out softly when Nathan proved to be far faster than she. An arm encircled her waist, bringing her to an abrupt halt midflight. She was held captive an instant before Nathan lightly tossed her, as if she weighed no more than a feather, back down onto the softness of mattress and pillow. She landed unhurt but with a sharp gasp and widening eyes. She could hardly believe what was happening. The tender lover Nathan had been last night seemed to have vanished completely to be replaced by . . . by an incensed man intent only on satisfying his own lusts. Kate's need to escape intensified, and when Nathan sat down on the edge of the bed, his gaze hard upon her, she flipped over and tried to roll to the side again. She succeeded in putting less distance between them than she had the last time, and with frighteningly little exertion on Nathan's part, he brought her down flat on the bed once more.

"Be still," he commanded brusquely, one hand gripping her waist as with the other he started to slowly undo the buttons of his shirt she was wearing. She tried to twist free. His grip on her tightened, and his eyes bored into the depths of hers, as he repeated through clenched teeth, "Dammit, be still, Katie. You're just wasting effort because you're not getting away from me. I told you I was going to erase Phillip and your guilt from your mind for the next several hours, and that's exactly what I plan to do. Starting now."

"But why, Nathan! *Why?*" she asked, cursing the slight shakiness she heard in her own voice, wanting to show him no more signs of weakness than she already had. To compensate for the tremulously spoken words, she forced a minute outjutting of her chin. Her eyes bored right back into his as she added with as much sarcasm as she could muster, "Why are you doing this? What am I? Some kind of challenge you can't resist?"

"Oh, hell, yes, Katie, you're a challenge. And no, I can't resist," he replied tauntingly, pulling the shirt completely off her. Then he slipped her shoes off, stripped her of her jeans, only smiling when she stiffened in passive resistance. With teasing procrastination, he removed her wispy white bra and panties, and at last, her naked body was exposed in all its enticingly curved glory. He swept a hand across her abdomen, and smiled faintly as the skimming touch caused a fluttering of muscles just beneath the surface of skin. "Umm, yes, love, you're such a delightful challenge."

A challenge to his male ego? Was that all she was to him? A nicely curved body he could overpower and use to reassert the male's dominion over women? Kate's heart ached with the possibility that he was going to use her to gratify mere physical needs and not consider her feelings one whit while doing it. Panic rose in her. She simply couldn't let him subject her to such a hurtful humiliating experience, even if she had to resort to begging and pleading to prevent his doing it. She tried to literally shrink away when his chest brushed her breasts as he lowered himself down, bracing on his elbows above her.

"Nathan, you can't! Don't hurt me this way," she exclaimed softly, meaning hurt more in the emotional sense than the physical. A haunted shadow darkened the fragile features of her face as she looked up at him. "Don't, Nathan. Don't hurt me."

"*Hurt you?*" Surprise showed in his lean face and suddenly his gaze, though still passionately intent and purposeful, gentled. He smiled again but not with mockery as he had previously. There was only the tiniest movement of carved lips, but the smile seemed vaguely reassuring. "Katie, *baby*, I'm not going to *hurt* you. I never intended to. What purpose would that serve? I couldn't drive Phillip out of your mind with pain. No, love, you're going to enjoy what we have together." He leaned down, brushed her hair back from her face, and nibbled teasingly on the tender flesh of one earlobe, then whispered coaxingly, "Relax. I promise the next few hours will bring you as much pleasure as they do me."

Kate still lay tensed beneath him, but as his firm caressing lips began to explore the shell-like contours of her ear, a suffusing warmth spread through her, easing some of the tension in her limbs. Nathan's breath drifted in her inner ear, causing her to shiver and tilt her head toward him. He trailed strands of lingering seductive kisses across her cheeks, the delicate edge of her jaw, and her forehead before his mouth sought, found, and covered hers with deepening rousing persuasion. Fear burned away in the wildfires he was kindling in her every nerve ending. Her lips parted and closed again on the fuller lower curve of his, and ever so slowly her hands slid up from against his chest to stroke and knead his shoulders. Then her arms were around him completely.

Even then, however, the last vestiges of a self-protective instinct clamored to be heard. Kate stiffened slightly, trying to will herself to be unresponsive. She shook her head. "I . . . can't just let you . . . use me. I . . ."

"I've never used you, Katie. I'm not using you now. You said yourself this is right for us, didn't you?" His lips touched the riotous pulse in her temples. "Didn't you?"

"Yes but . . ."

"No more talk," he muttered, catching up the remainder of her protest in a kiss. Kate struggled a bit then was still when Nathan lifted his head to smile lazily down at her. One fingertip traced the graceful natural arch of her eyebrows and brushed the tips of thick feathery lashes, causing her eyes to flutter shut while she gave a tremulous sigh. He followed the line of her jaw from the tender fleshy lobe of one ear to the other. He touched the tip of her small nose, high contouring cheekbones, and finally, the corners of her mouth. The tactile exploration of her face was incredibly effective. His finesse was arousing her to incredible heights, and he had to know that because Kate had begun to tremble and not from fear. His touch was such a delight that she didn't think of resisting when he rather impatiently tossed back the rumpled sheet with which she had earlier tried to cover herself.

Kate's eyes opened briefly when he turned her over onto her stomach, but she closed them again and swallowed back a soft moan as his lips blazed a searing trail of fire over creamy shoulders that continued down the length of her spine to the hollow of the arch that flared out into the curve of firm round hips. His hands began a caressing massage of her back, fingertips grazing the taut sides of her breasts then sliding down to the astoundingly sensitive skin of her bare waist. Kate was rapidly losing the battle of maintaining even the pretense of resistence and feigned indifference was soon out of the question too. Streaks of tingling electricity seemed to be shooting over her skin from the tips of her toes to the top of her head, and she could no longer hold back a shuddery gasp of pleasure when Nathan's caressing massage expanded to include scattered nibbling kisses.

By the time Nathan turned Kate over onto her back again, she was all warmth and femininely acquiescent. Her arms came up to encircle his shoulders while his parted lips took firm possession of hers. She watched with half-closed eyes when he lowered his head and ran the tip of his tongue around the circle of her naval. She felt the curving of his smile as her stomach muscles involuntarily rippled and contracted, and he heard her swiftly indrawn breath. Even as her small fingers tangled feverishly in his hair, he turned his head to gaze deeply into her eyes.

"Massage my back too, Katie," he murmured, the statement an evocative demand. And when he moved to lie on his stomach, Kate sat up, a strange excitement mounting in her with the realization that she was more than willing to concede to that demand. She knelt beside him, only half aware of the hushed silence in the room, as she bemusedly surveyed the superbly masculine lineation of his lithe body. Her fingers suddenly ached to touch that broad expanse of brown skin. Leaning over him, her hair falling forward in a silken curtain around her face, she laid her hands on him, tentatively at first then with increasing confidence. She lightly massaged his shoulders until corded muscles flexed somewhat demandingly.

"A little harder wouldn't hurt, love," Nathan whispered, deep amusement in his low voice. "I won't break, I promise."

As he watched her out of the corner of his eye, she had to smile, and after giving him a playful little nudge with the heel of one hand, she proceeded to knead his back and shoulders with a much firmer, deeply stroking touch. All in all, she enjoyed playing the masseuse as much as he seemed to enjoy her doing it. There was a great appeal in having some control over him rather than it being the other way around. She soon discovered, however, the lethargy the massage seemed to be inducing in him was deceptive to say the very least. She had just drawn the backs of her fingers down the length of his spine and started to begin again when he abruptly turned over, reached up, and pulled her down on top of him.

"*Nathan!*" she gasped with a sharp expulsion of her breath. "What . . ."

"You're driving me crazy, touching me like that," he murmured, smiling rather wickedly, looking into the face so close to his. "But you know what you do to me, don't you?"

Before Kate could deny that, he cupped the back of her head in one hand, holding her fast, drawing her closer still until her lips were touching his. And from the moment his hard mouth took hers with nearly bruising, slightly twisting pressure, she was certain of the power she had over him. She wasn't sorry that her caresses elicited such a demanding response from him. The kisses they exchanged had freed her from some of the restraints she had always imposed on herself. With a murmur of satisfaction, she wrapped her slender arms around his neck, eager to feel the pillowed softness of her breasts yield to the firm plane of his chest. The weight of the full length of her slight body rested on him, and she was fluidly pliant when his hand on her rounded hips pressed her demandingly between his long legs. Rigid strength surged against her, and she whispered his name throatily in the hollow beneath his jaw.

"Katie, *Katie,*" he muttered roughly, turning with one quick motion to bring her beneath him. He looked down at the satin-sheened breasts straining against his chest and bent his head further to stroke his lips over the upswelling curves of tight flesh. He blew a gently teasing breath into the shadowed valley between her breasts, and when Kate's hands moved probingly over his broad back, he kissed her many times, each kiss more deeply seeking as he relentlessly pursued his quest to drive everything from her mind except him. He had more than succeeded even before he slowly, reluctantly released her mouth to gaze searchingly into the bottomless emerald depths of eyes aglow with ardor.

"No other man has ever seen you like this," he said, his voice barely a rough whisper. He brushed a tendril of hair back from her right temple. "That means you're mine, Katie. And I'm going to prove that to you right now."

The mere promise was enough to make her breathing quickening and her senses reel. She *was* his in many more ways than merely the physical sense, but if he only wanted possession of her body now, she was too weakened by love and expertly aroused desire to prevent him from doing with her anything he wished. There was a tiny uprising of fear in her because she was once again becoming so vulnerable to him, yet even that fear was almost immediately overpowered by another ravishing kiss that quickly banished all thought from her mind. He had swept her up into that world again where she could only feel joy at being with him. Conquered by a woman's uncontrollable love, Kate signaled surrender with a slow trembling breath as he moved gently over her and made her his.

It was much much later when Kate lay in Nathan's light embrace, and she wouldn't have cared if she never had to move out of his arms. He had promised bliss, but what they had shared, for her at least, had transcended the heights of ecstasy. There had been something much more spiritual in her giving of herself to him; she had felt a true sense of belonging which lingered even now as his heartbeat slowed to normal beneath her hand curled on his chest. She couldn't regret either last night or today. Later, perhaps she might, but right now, she wouldn't allow herself to give in to her innermost fear that she was indeed only a challenge Nathan felt compelled to meet. For that reason, she lay very quiet and still, unwilling to break the magic spell the past few hours had woven around her. Soon she could tell by the slow even tenor of Nathan's breathing that he had fallen asleep and she, too, gave in to a contented drowsiness and drifted off into a dream. In the beginning the scene that unfolded in her mind's eye was pleasant. She was at Ten Oaks, walking through a wood near the house, but after a short while, a sense of foreboding built in her with every step she took. And, unhappily, dreams sometimes mirror the very fears most fervently suppressed during waking hours. Kate's dream became painful. She needed to be with Nathan and was searching for him everywhere, but when she found him at last, he showed little interest in being with her. He was polite as one might be to a very casual acquaintance, and Kate began to *feel* his indifference, to *know* he scarcely remembered all they had once shared. A keen sense of aloneness assailed her. A horrible sadness settled heavily in her chest and lingered in a dull ache even after she dragged herself awake. She was in Nathan's bed; his arms were around her yet she was afraid. Compulsively, she touched light fingertips to his face. He roused enough to smile lazily and run a hand over her rumpled hair, as any man might touch any woman he had just shared hours of intimacy with. The seemingly careless caress wasn't enough to reassure Kate.

"Hold me," she whispered, her hand slipping up his chest to curve over one shoulder. "Hold me closer, Nathan."

Coming more fully awake, he did as she asked, turning onto

his side to draw her tightly against him. His lips grazed her forehead as he murmured, "What's wrong, Katie?"

She shrugged lightly. "Bad dream, I guess."

"What about?"

"I don't really remember," she lied. "Just something that made me feel a little sad, but it's all right now."

Nathan said nothing else but continued to hold her for several minutes. Then, still in silence, he moved away and got up, leaving her alone in his bed. He looked back down at her. "Hungry, Katie?"

Her gaze captured by the impenetrable expression in his, she nodded and smiled faintly. "Now that you mention it, I think I am, a little."

"I know I am. And after we have something to eat, we'll leave for Charlotte to make it there by early this evening. Give you a chance to settle in and relax tonight. After all, tomorrow's your big day."

"Yes," she murmured. But it wasn't her new position in the main office she was thinking about when her eyes followed Nathan across the room. The door of the adjoining bath closed behind him. She heard the spray of the shower. Nuzzling her cheek against his pillow, she could detect the lingering scent of lime after shave. Although she still felt no regret about what had happened between them this weekend, she couldn't entirely eliminate a nagging little fear. In the hope that whatever Nathan felt for her now could eventually become love, she was taking a risk. She, who for the past six years had practically programmed every aspect of her life as if she were a computer, had suddenly become a gambler. She could only say a silent prayer that she would win out in the end. But what if she didn't?

CHAPTER SEVEN

Charlotte had changed since Kate had last seen it. New, modern buildings of concrete and glass had sprung up across the city, yet Kate recognized enough familiar landmarks to prevent her feeling like a foreign visitor. She also realized they were heading away from downtown rather than toward it when Nathan exited the interstate to take a street that meandered through one of the most prestigious residential districts.

"Didn't you tell me your secretary reserved a room for me in the Lee Plaza?" Kate questioned, unconsciously tucking her legs up to one side of her when she turned in her seat to look at Nathan. "I remember that's downtown, near the store, so why are we heading this way?"

Nathan glanced from the road at her, a smile appearing on his tanned face as he cocked one dark eyebrow. "You don't seem particularly alarmed that we're going in the wrong direction. In that comfortable position, you don't look like you're having ideas about trying to jump from the car."

A puzzled frown wrinkled Kate's brow. "Why in the world *should* I have ideas like that? I simply asked why we're heading

122

this way. Did it sound like I thought you were kidnapping me or something?"

"Maybe." He glanced from the road at her again. "After this weekend, you could be thinking anything. Maybe you've told yourself that, at best, I'm a seducer of young women. Have you, Katie?"

"No," was her candid answer, but she turned her head away, aware of the warmth gathering in her cheeks as she stared blindly out her window. He *had* seduced her, but she had been such a willing participant in the seduction. She would never be able to lie to herself and pretend it had been different. Nathan had taken nothing from her she hadn't wanted to give, and knowing he knew that, she could only surmise he wanted to be certain she viewed the weekend as realistically. Now she had admitted she did, yet was unwilling to discuss the subject further. This afternoon's disturbing dream had reminded her all too vividly of the potential heartache she was risking by acknowledging to herself how very much she loved him still. Unable to cope with her fears as yet, she wanted only to push them far back in her mind and could hardly do that if she and Nathan discussed the weekend they'd just shared. For her own peace of mind, she steered the conversation back to where it had begun originally. "You never did say why we're heading this way," she murmured without looking directly at Nathan again. "I know your parents' house is in this area, but you told me they're in Europe."

"They are, but my house is a couple of miles beyond theirs, farther out in the country."

Kate's green eyes were alight with interest as they briefly met his. "You have your own home now? That must be nice. It just never occurred to me you weren't still living with your family."

Nathan assumed the most horrified expression he could. "You must be kidding, Katie! I couldn't stay with them. Had to have my own pad for the wild, free-swinging bachelor's life I'm living."

Kate wrinkled her nose at him, knowing he was kidding. Six

years might have passed, but Nathan's personality couldn't have changed that drastically. He knew how to have fun, yes, but he also knew how to be serious too. And he had never ever been superficial nor was he now. For him life could never be just one perpetual quest for the high old time. He owned his own home for something far more precious to him. Her warm gaze roamed over him, loving him, understanding him. Obviously sensing she was watching him, he looked once more at her, and she smiled softly. "You always needed a certain amount of solitude, didn't you, Nathan?"

The strangest light flared in his aqua eyes, an indefinable light. Reaching across the seat, he rubbed the back of his hand over a creamy cheek. "You see, Katie, you do remember something about what I'm really like. Don't you, although you'll rarely admit it?"

Kate didn't have time to decipher the cryptic comment or even complete a request for an explanation. "I don't think I know what you meant by that. I . . ."

"Never mind," he interrupted, gesturing toward the gentle curve in the oak-lined road before them. "We're almost there. You'll like my house. Trees all around it. Since it's only a little after seven, I decided you'd rather come here and have dinner before checking into the hotel. That place is going to become tiresome if it takes you awhile to find an apartment."

Kate nodded but felt somewhat uneasy. Loving Nathan the way she did, she was quite naturally eager to see the place in which he lived, yet she wondered at the wisdom of going there with him. A few short hours ago they had been making love. No one else in the world had existed, and she couldn't forget how enticing sharing that exclusive world with him had been. In his home she might be tempted to once again . . . No! She was stronger willed than that. Recognizing her own confused state of mind, she knew she needed time to think about Nathan rationally. Even in his home, she simply wouldn't allow herself to be tempted. Yet . . .

Kate's aggravating vacillation of feelings came to an abrupt halt the moment Nathan swung the Jaguar off the road onto a paved drive, tunneled by overhanging branches of maple trees. At once, Kate's inner conflict was temporarily forgotten as she sat up straighter in her seat, almost breathlessly awaiting the first glimpse of Nathan's house. She wasn't disappointed in what she saw. Nestled in the trees, the varnished cedarwood house was on two levels, and at the end of the upper, a circular deck extended out practically into the treetops. Kate loved it instantly. It blended so unobtrusively into the surroundings it almost seemed as if it had sprung up magically.

When Kate and Nathan went inside a moment later, she found the interior as appealing as the exterior was. A vast stone fireplace was the focal point in a sprawling den decorated in ice blues, muted reds, and ivory. The furnishings were all simple pieces with those clean lines and fine craftsmanship that bespoke elegance but not opulence. Turning around in the center of the large room, Kate took in everything, clasped her hands together, and announced enthusiastically, "Oh, Nathan, I love this! Would you show me the rest of the house, please?"

After a tour of the spacious kitchen and Nathan's large but cozy study downstairs, he led her to the upper level with its four bedrooms. A door at the end of the hallway opened onto the circular deck but two of the rooms also had private access. The second of these was the master suite, done in rich earth tones that were warm and mellow and contrasted prettily with the lush green of the trees overhanging the deck outside the French windows. Kate glanced at the exceptionally large bath then wandered back through the dressing room with its mirrored walls. She stopped automatically to slowly turn around as she inspected her simply cut green linen dress for wrinkles. Smoothing her hair, rather windswept from the ride with the windows down, she looked up and found Nathan leaning in the doorway, watching. She grinned.

"A person could become a real narcissus in here. Or a bar

could be put up all around, and it would become a terrific place to do ballet exercises." She went to him, looking up with a mischievous sparkle in her eyes. "I bet you never knew that when I was a kid, I was certain a room like this could have made me a prima ballerina. Of course, now I realize it takes a bit of talent too."

"In some ways, you haven't changed much in six years, Katie. There's still that intriguing glimpse of the little girl in you," he said with somewhat disturbing solemnity, his piercing eyes plumbing the depths of hers for several spellbinding seconds. Then he smiled easily and the spell, if Kate hadn't simply imagined it, was broken as if it had never existed. Hands in his pockets, he escorted her back across the bedroom but stopped at the doorway. "Would you like to sit out on the deck for a while or have something to eat first? My housekeeper doesn't live in, but she always leaves something delicious in the refrigerator for Sunday evening."

Kate glanced toward the French doors. The deck did look so serenely inviting. "I don't suppose," she began hopefully, "that we could have dinner up here, on the deck, I mean? Or would that be a great deal of trouble?"

"Not particularly. A stairway outside the kitchen door leads up to the deck. If you don't mind carrying up what we need . . ."

"Oh, I won't. Will you? Let's do it," Kate urged, her enthusiasm infectious, and when he nodded agreeably, renewed contentment dissipated her fears for the time being. Maybe it was being in Nathan's hideaway home with him that created such a comforting sense of belonging. She wasn't sure why she felt the way she did. She only knew it was a feeling she wanted to hold on to for as long as possible.

Dinner consisted of shrimp salad remoulade served with white wine and the fresh watercress salad Kate prepared. It was a light meal but satisfying and Kate especially enjoyed dining at the small round table beneath the overhanging branch of an ancient

126

oak. She could practically reach up and touch the leaves. Dusk was darkening into night, however; the surrounding wood lay in black shadow and only post lamps situated strategically along the edge of the deck provided soft illumination. Much as Kate hated the idea of the unexpectedly relaxing evening ending, she knew it must. With an inward sigh, she got up from the table and began to gather up the dishes.

"I'll help you tidy up down in the kitchen," she said, unaware of the hint of regret in her soft tone. "Then I think I should get to the hotel and check in."

Nathan simply nodded, stood, then carried the tray down the stairs. In short order, the kitchen was made neat again, and after Kate tucked away the last salad plate into the appropriate cupboard, Nathan put a hand on her shoulder to turn her round to face him. Long fingers glided into the thick silkiness of her hair and he tilted her head back slightly.

"You really don't have to go to the hotel," he said very quietly, his deep voice almost a caress in itself. "You could stay here with me."

Kate could feel herself becoming lost in the mesmerizing light in his eyes, and for a weak instant, she was tempted to accept his invitation. Yet, delightful as their evening had been, she recalled the afternoon doubts she had experienced, and she knew herself well enough to realize she needed time to think. She had already placed her emotions in enough jeopardy this weekend; now warning signals were sounding in her head. If she plunged headlong into an intense affair with Nathan, an affair that would probably be no more than a casual interlude for him, she might never be able to totally alleviate the pain that would come when everything between them ended. Before she should even think of becoming involved in a situation like that, she needed time alone to thoroughly consider *all* the possible hurtful consequences. Still looking up at Nathan, she at last shook her head.

"I have to go to the hotel," she told him decisively. "I really couldn't . . . *can't* stay here." She forced a nonchalant smile. "If

I spent the night with you, someone at the office might find out. What would people think?"

"*What would people think?*" Nathan lifted his eyes heavenward in mock exasperation. "It seems to me I've heard that song before. Obviously, you hate the thought of being gossiped about as much as ever. But why then didn't you seem to mind if fellow employees knew you were seeing Joe?"

She shrugged. "Joe wasn't my boss."

Dark eyebrows lifted. "Yes, Katie, he was your immediate supervisor."

She hesitated, mulled that over a second, and shrugged again. "I guess I just didn't feel like he was my boss."

"But you feel like I am?"

"Nathan, you own the whole damn chain of stores! Of course I feel like you're my boss . . . maybe employer is a better word. Anyway, I doubt people thought I was seeing Joe to further my career. But you've just promoted me and brought me to Charlotte, and if I were to spend my very first night here with you, everyone would . . ." Her words trailed off at the muted sound of his low laughter.

"You can be so enchantingly intent," he said, surveying her with indulgent amusement. With a fingertip he gently tapped the end of her small nose then took her arm. "Come along, Katie. I'll drive you to the hotel right now. You're right about office gossip. We really shouldn't risk it."

His nonchalant acceptance of her refusal to spend the night with him rankled a little, but Kate was mildly irritated at herself for feeling even that tiny bit of resentment. When they drove away from his house a few minutes later, she knew she should really be relieved that he didn't seem to care whether or not she stayed with him. Yet, somehow, she wasn't at all relieved.

Traffic in Charlotte proper was light, and Nathan easily found a parking space directly across the street from the prestigious Lee Plaza Hotel.

"You could have just let me off at the entrance," Kate said as he expertly maneuvered the Jaguar into the space between two other vehicles. "I only have two bags and the doorman would help me with them. You don't have to go to the trouble of going in with me."

"If I'd felt like it was too much trouble, Katie, I'd have called a taxi to bring you here," Nathan said flatly as he switched off the powerful engine. He got out of the car, came round to her side to open her door, and took her hand as she stepped out onto the curb. His smile was vaguely teasing. "And furthermore, my mother taught me it was the height of bad manners to take a lady to a hotel and just push her out of the car at the entrance. A true gentleman accompanies the lady inside."

"Such chivalry," Kate replied pertly but found herself returning his smile. It suddenly struck her as amazing that sometimes the two of them could be so perfectly at ease with each other, while at others, mutual tension seemed to swirl about them like a thick miasmic cloud. Pondering the terrific highs and dismal lows of their relationship, Kate watched as Nathan removed her luggage from the trunk of the car.

The lobby of the Plaza was so plushly elegant that Kate knew Nathan was going to great expense to provide accommodations for her there. She started to say that a much less exorbitant motel room would have sufficed but decided against it. Such a statement would undoubtedly prompt another rather comical dissertation on what his mother thought constituted good manners. While Kate signed the register, Nathan watched, and when she finished, it was at him the very eager-to-please desk clerk smiled obsequiously.

"We'll of course do everything we possibly can to make Miss Austin's stay here with us as pleasant as possible," the clerk babbled. "Should she need anything, she only has to ask."

"Yes, I assumed that," Nathan drawled, looking around expectantly.

Taking the hint, the clerk sharply slapped the bell on the desk, and a bellman rushed from around the corner to carefully swoop up Kate's luggage. As he accepted the room key from the clerk, Kate smiled up at Nathan, trying not to appear as uncertain as she felt now that their weekend was truly at an end. "I assume personnel's still located in the same place at the store?" she inquired, nodding after he did. "Then I guess I'll see you tomorrow."

"Don't say good night just yet, Katie. I'm going to see you up to your room. Remember? Chivalry isn't dead," he told her, inclining his head toward the bellman who led them toward the bank of elevators in an alcove off the lobby. They were zipped up to the seventh floor where Nathan inexplicably tipped the bellman at the elevator, took Kate's luggage from him, then carried it to the door of her room himself. He turned the key in the lock, pushed the door open, but blocked Kate's way when she started to go in.

"Just let me have a quick glance around first," he murmured mysteriously.

"But Nathan, this hotel has an excellent reputation! You don't really think someone might be lurking around in there?"

"Indulge me, Katie," he commanded softly, slipping into the dark room to flip up the light switch. "Some of the better hotels in Charlotte have been hit by a jewel thief recently."

Kate followed, laughing. "Well, he won't get much if he decides to rob me."

"He wouldn't know that, though, would he?"

Kate's smile faded, but then the thief was forgotten as she realized they had entered an elegantly furnished sitting room. "You reserved a suite! Nathan, you didn't have to do that. I didn't expect . . ."

"I didn't give you time enough to come here and find an apartment, and if that takes a few weeks, you'll be more comfortable in a suite. Less confined than you would be in a single room."

Kate looked around. "Well, it's certainly luxurious. More

luxurious than any apartment I can afford will be. Maybe I won't look very hard and just stay here."

Nathan smiled but the smile was subdued. His expression was more somber now than it had been, and he raked his fingers through his dark hair, something he rarely did. Obviously in no hurry to leave, he seemed on the verge of saying something yet didn't say it. Then he noticed Kate's questioning stare, took one small hand in both his, and drew her onto the sofa beside him as he sat down.

"Katie, I have something unpleasant to tell you."

Her mouth went dry and it was difficult to swallow. Her heart sank. Suddenly she felt weighted down with dread, although she really had no idea what he was about to say. Her heartbeat accelerated and her breathing became increasingly shallow with every second she waited for him to continue. Then something terrifying occurred to her: what if Evelyn had been right? What if Nathan was now going to tell her that he was engaged again to Lydia? Kate tried to steel herself for that possibility, vowing to show no reaction if indeed that was what he had to say. But he still said nothing. He simply looked at her, an uncertainty she had never seen before in him playing over his rugged features. Finally, she could no longer bear the suspense.

"Well, Nathan?" she prompted, her voice surprisingly steady. "What is it?"

"It's something about Phillip."

Phillip. He was going to tell her something about Phillip, not Lydia! Kate was nearly light-headed with relief but managed to conceal that reaction too. At last she was able to take a truly deep breath again. "What about Phillip?"

"I was never going to tell you this. I decided long ago that it would be pointless to and might actually make matters worse," Nathan said, playing idly with her fingertips. "But now I think I have to chance that because of the nightmare you had this afternoon, the nightmare about Phillip."

Kate quickly glanced down at his hands holding her own,

unable to meet his eyes directly. She wanted to deny her dream had been about Phillip yet pride wouldn't allow her to reveal the truth, that she had dreamed he had lost all interest in her and awakened heartsick and clinging to him? To do that would be comparable to simply blurting out her love for him. She would only embarrass him and humiliate herself and that she would *not* do. "I still don't understand," she murmured instead. "What haven't you told me about Phillip?"

"Katie, he was seen out with other girls after the two of you became engaged," Nathan said grimly, his free hand coming up to cup her face. He rubbed the edge of his thumb across her cheek, as if he meant his touch to be consoling as he added, "In fact, he was seen frequently, usually on nights when you had a class."

Kate stared at him incredulously, her mouth moving but no sounds issuing forth from it. After several seconds, she recovered her voice. "But that's preposterous! Phillip wouldn't have done that. I don't believe a word of it. It's crazy."

Nathan's eyes narrowed. "I've never lied to you, Katie."

"I'm not accusing *you* of lying now. Maybe you believe the people who told you these stories but I don't. I'll never believe Phillip went out with other girls after we were engaged. That's all there is to it."

"But, for God's sake, Katie, I *saw* . . ."

"Why are you telling me this now?" she asked bewilderedly, hearing nothing of what he'd started saying. "If you believed all this six years ago, why didn't you tell me then?"

"I didn't tell you because, first of all, you weren't being very reasonable about anything at the time. I knew you wouldn't listen. Secondly, Phillip had been my friend. I didn't especially relish the idea of being the one to tell you he'd cheated on you, not one time but many. But if I had known you were going to drag this guilt around with you all these years, I wouldn't have hesitated to tell you. I wish I had now. Maybe after hearing the truth, you couldn't have gone on thinking he'd killed himself because you broke your engagement."

"But it can't be true," Kate protested vehemently, thinking Nathan would say anything to conquer her, to break her down. "Phillip loved me. Or at least he thought he did, which amounts to the same thing."

"Damn, you're impossible!" Nathan growled, impatience and anger flaring hotly in his eyes and tightening his features into harsh lines. His hands closed around her upper arms, fingers biting into flesh. "Katie, you look back at Phillip through rose-tinted glasses, never admitting or even recognizing that he had faults. But he did, and you've got to end this self-tormenting guilt trip." With a muffled exclamation, he hauled her close to him but when he covered her mouth with his, he wasn't rough as she had expected his anger to make him be. Instead, his lips were hard yet persuasively gentle and the deepening kiss evoked the memory of the intimate hours they had spent together the past two days. For a long time there was silence in the room then he held her away from him. Desire heightened the angry flame in his searching gaze. "You weren't thinking about Phillip then. And you didn't think about him this afternoon, did you, Katie?"

"No," she admitted breathlessly. "You said you'd make me forget him and you succeeded."

"Yes. I thought I did. But what the hell am I supposed to do? Keep you in bed with me every minute of every day? I'd be delighted, if that were possible, but it isn't. But somehow I'm going to see to it that you finally understand completely that we did nothing wrong six years ago. I've had enough of your feeling ashamed of what happened between us."

"Why does it matter?" she asked as he stood and glowered down at her. She nibbled her lower lip, confused by the extent of his anger. "Why do you care how I feel?"

"You said it yourself. You're a challenge I can't resist," he answered bluntly. Leaving her, he strode to the door but paused to look back. A sardonic smile moved his mouth. "Just remem-

133

ber, Katie, I never back away from a challenge, and I never quit until the objective's achieved. No matter how hard you fight me, I'm going to win."

Kate breathed a deep shuddering sigh as Nathan left and the door closed behind him. She stretched out on the sofa, burrowing her face in a round velvet corner pillow. She was a challenge, an achievable objective, and he was determined to exorcise all her guilt about Phillip's death. Little did he know that it was not really Phillip's ghost but the specter of loneliness she would have to face when she was no longer even a challenge to him that haunted her now.

CHAPTER EIGHT

Wednesday evening, Nathan invited Gary Roberts and his wife, Helen, and Kate to his house for dinner. It was an occasion designed to help Kate and Gary become better acquainted, arranged because that past weekend had been a very busy one for Kate. In the rental car provided by the store until she brought hers from Raleigh, Kate drove to the house secluded in the trees, anticipating the evening ahead. She had liked Gary Roberts almost from the first moment they had met Monday morning. In his mid-fifties, Gary wasn't frantic to scramble up the corporate ladder, careless of whose fingers he trod on in the process. He was more the relaxed executive, confident of his abilities, hardworking, and extremely competent. And, thus far, he had shown absolutely no impatience as Kate tried to become acclimated to her new working environment and more extensive job responsibilities. Also, Gary appealed to Kate on the personal level. Unabashedly a family man, he doted on his wife, two children, and grandchildren. The warmth of his happy home life spilled over to include the people with whom he worked. Kate was certain she would enjoy being his assistant and looked forward this evening to meeting Helen, who was apparently one terrific lady, judging by the fond comments Gary had made about her.

Much as Kate admired Gary, however, she realized it was actually Nathan she was eager to see at tonight's small dinner party. Since Sunday, she had only seen him a few times at the office, and there his manner toward her was strictly professional and always courteous. Of course, she preferred it that way. These were her first days in a new job, and he would have added considerably to her nervousness if he'd given her fellow employees an indication that they also had a personal relationship. Still, the distance he had put between them had made Kate rather lonely for the Nathan who teased her, touched her, and made her feel more vitally alive than any other man ever had. This evening, in his home again, she hoped he would be more like that Nathan once more, instead of merely Mr. Cordell, her employer.

As Kate turned off the road onto Nathan's tree-edged drive, the excitement that had been rising in her all day became more intense. Smoothing her hair as she parked in front of the rustic house, she noticed happily that except for Nathan's Jaguar, no other cars were there. Apparently Gary and Helen hadn't arrived yet, and she experienced only the tiniest twinge of guilt for being secretly elated that she would have at least a few minutes alone with Nathan before they came.

Out of her car she smoothed the softly shirred skirt of her rose georgette dress, then went to the door to lightly tap the hammer against the brass knocker. Several moments later, the door was opened, Nathan reached out, and unceremoniously ushered her into the foyer. Before she uttered a word, he took her purse and laid it on a side table.

"Glad you're here," he said, rushing her along through the spacious den. "I certainly need some help in the kitchen."

"So that's the only reason you invited me," said Kate with an exaggerated sigh of disappointment. "If I'd known you were going to appoint me chief cook and bottle washer, I . . ."

"Correction. *I'm* chief cook. I might let you be bottle washer later. Right now I just need some assistance," he told her, opening a drawer to remove a frilly little organdy apron. "Mother insists I keep this here for her, and it'll come in handy for you." Deftly slipping the apron strings around Kate's waist, he tied them in back. His hands moved to her sides to linger, following her insweeping shape as he softly said, "You're particularly lovely tonight, Katie. So lovely that I have to do now what I've wanted to do every time I've seen you in the office this week."

Kate went into his arms eagerly, her parted lips meeting his, and it was as if they had hungered for each other for weeks, months, even years instead of a mere three days. He gathered her so tightly to him that her slender frame was arched back against strong supportive arms, but as love's passion began smoldering in her then caught fire, she felt she could never be close enough to him. Wild currents, jolting as the touch of a live electric wire, rushed over her. She trembled, feeling the quickening beat of his heart against her breasts. Her arms were around his neck, her fingers tangling in his hair while he pushed back the silken swathe that brushed her neck and kissed the throbbing pulse he found there. Kate's breath caught audibly when even teeth nibbled gently at a tender morsel of creamy skin, and it was then that Nathan lifted his head, though reluctantly, to cup her face in his hands.

Her eyes met his. The all-consuming flame of passion in the aqua depths made coherent thought difficult. Her limbs went weak with her aching need to be kissed again, but Nathan's scorching gaze was so intense it threatened to burn away all consideration of here and now. And now was when dinner guests were expected to arrive. Resolutely, Kate tried to take control of the situation. She lowered her gaze to the bronzed V of skin exposed where his shirt collar was open. A faint smile curved her lips.

"I don't think I expected this," she murmured. "At the office the last three days, you haven't acted at all like you wanted to kiss me."

"You've never known what a consummate actor I can be, have you, Katie?"

"No. And I don't know it now. Maybe you told me you'd been wanting to kiss me simply to have something provocative to say."

"Katie, you do love to live dangerously." With the swiftness of a swooping hawk, he kissed her again and muttered between a series of deepening possessions of her mouth, "Does this really feel like mere provocation?"

It didn't. The entire length of his body, his hard lips, his exploring hands all conveyed a nearly intolerable level of a man's desire. He wanted her; Kate couldn't deny that but desire isn't love, and love was what she needed from him. Yet even that nagging reality barely enabled her to escape succumbing to his dizzying touch and caressing kisses. With the very last of her will power, she freed her lips from the hard marauding pressure of his.

"Gary and his wife could get here any minute," she whispered breathlessly, moving her hands down to press them against his chest. "Think how shocked they'd be to find us like this."

"Surprised, maybe. Shocked, no," Nathan said gruffly. He released her with a decisive nod. "But you're right. Since we can't finish this now, we shouldn't begin. Besides, dinner's already going to be a little late. An emergency came up at the office, and I didn't get home as early as I'd planned." He motioned toward the refrigerator. "That's why you've been drafted. You do the salad while I see to everything else."

"I had no idea you were making dinner tonight," Kate remarked, taking the romaine and other fixings from the vegetable crisper. "Actually, I had no idea you could cook."

"There's a great deal you don't seem to know about me," he replied but without any real undercurrent of tension. "But bachelors either learn to cook or they practically starve. Luckily,

138

I can fend for myself when Stella, my housekeeper, can't stay to prepare dinner. She couldn't stay tonight. I decided on steak."

"Umm, steak's a safe choice," Katie murmured, a barely discernible sparkle of amusement dancing in her eyes as they met his across the kitchen. "Most people like steak."

His gaze narrowed speculatively; he almost smiled. "All right, I admit it won't be the most imaginative meal you've ever eaten. But I never claimed to be a gourmet."

"Oh, but I love steak," Kate countered innocently, failing to bend her head quickly enough to prevent him from seeing her widening grin.

The light-spirited banter between Nathan and Kate continued even after Gary and his wife arrived. Dinner was relaxing, enjoyable; Kate made a point of complimenting Nathan on the truly delicious steak he had prepared, receiving a nod and a wry smile in response. Later, Kate stayed in the kitchen with Nathan to make coffee and cut portions of the strawberry torte Stella had made earlier in the day. When she served Helen and Gary, who waited in the den, she suddenly realized she had become the unofficial hostess of this dinner party. That realization was not displeasing, and she was warmed by that odd sense of belonging again when she and Nathan automatically paired together on the love seat facing the sofa the older couple had taken.

Conversation was general, pointedly steered by Nathan away from business. He had said he wanted Kate and Gary to become better acquainted, and indeed, the evening was a social event. Kate could truly relax. She found she was as drawn to Gary's wife as strongly as she had been drawn to him. Helen was a genuinely pleasant person, witty, intelligent, and quite naturally curious. Kate's only tense moment came when she caught Helen's speculative gaze drift from Nathan to her then back to him again. She seemed to be wondering why the president of a department store chain was entertaining the newest junior member of his staff in his own home. When Nathan absently stretched out his arm on the back of the love seat behind Kate and his fingertips happened to graze her shoulder, Helen gave the younger woman a pleased, knowing smile. Kate smiled back, no longer tense. No matter what Helen thought about her relationship with Nathan, she wasn't the type of woman to go around gossiping about the two of them.

The evening slipped by quickly. It was eleven when conversation suddenly ceased as everyone heard Nathan's front door open and close, followed by footsteps in the foyer.

"What the devil?" Nathan muttered with a deepening frown, but before he could rise from the love seat, Lydia Clark Plemmons appeared in the den, an instantaneous smile appearing on her rose-glossed lips when she saw Nathan.

"Darling, I didn't realize you had guests until I drove up to the house; then I just decided I might as well come in," she explained, eyes only for him as she quickened her pace to cross the room. Lovely blond hair bounced prettily against her shoulders with every long graceful step she took, and she familiarly put her hands in Nathan's when he and Gary automatically stood. Flexing one leg at the knee, she raised up to press her lushly colored lips to Nathan's in a kiss which lingered much longer than a mere friendly peck would have. She at last settled back down on both elegantly shod feet. Sparing not even a glance in Kate's direction, she looked at Gary and smiled sweetly. "Oh, do sit down, Gary. You too, Nathan. I'll sit beside you. I didn't mean to interrupt your evening, but I knew you wouldn't mind if I came on in."

Kate minded when Lydia squeezed herself onto the small love seat, forcing her to move so close against the end that her hipbone dug into the upholstery until she could feel the wooden frame. To add insult to injury, Nathan didn't seem to mind at all that Lydia had simply invited herself in. Smiling down at his former fiancée, who was snuggled tight up beside him, he complimented her on her expensively tailored grass green linen slacks and silk print blouse.

"Thank you, darling." She laughed up at him. "I bought both

140

the slacks and the blouse at Cordell's this afternoon. How could you not like them? While I was in the store, I ran up to your office, but you were out." She moved her lips into a tiny pout, which she turned on Gary too. "I didn't see you either, Gary, and I did try to find you. I haven't seen you in so long. Or you, Helen. How are you?"

After the social amenities were exchanged, Nathan drew Lydia's attention to Kate with a casual, "You remember Kate Austin, don't you, Lydia?"

Lydia leaned forward slightly to look at the younger woman. To her credit, she smiled, and it was understandable, due to past circumstances, that warm sentiment was not mirrored in her clear brown eyes. "Of course, Miss Austin, I certainly do remember you," she drawled. "And I'd heard you were back in Charlotte. Working at the store again, I believe?"

Kate nodded. Her smile felt amazingly natural. "Yes, I'm at the store again. And how are you, Mrs. Plemmons?"

"I dropped the Plemmons after my divorce. I use my maiden name, Clark, again now," Lydia pronounced, even her forced smile fading a bit. Her gaze went cooler, almost iced, as she swept it over Kate. "I'm quite fine, thank you. But tell me about yourself. Which department at the store are you working in?"

"Katie's Gary's new assistant director in personnel," Nathan interceded, his smile including both young women. "That was her position at Renaldo's in Raleigh, and after we bought that store, I decided she deserved a promotion to the main office here."

"Oh, how nice. It must be so gratifying to move up in your career," Lydia said, her voice warmer but not her eyes. "I own a precious little antique shop on the outskirts of Charlotte, and oh, I do enjoy my work. Especially since I'm my own boss."

"Nathan's mine," Kate said dryly, ignoring the highly amused glances shot at her by Nathan, Helen, and Gary. "He and, of course, Gary. As bosses go, I certainly could have done much worse. And have, on occasion."

Lydia's smile was now nonexistent. Her pretty facial features hardened. "You seem to make a habit of working for Nathan though, don't you, Miss Austin. You worked for him six years ago too."

"Yes, I did."

"But you quit your job and left Charlotte very abruptly, didn't you?"

Kate took a long slow breath. How long was this charade of an inquisition going to last? Lydia knew very well that Kate had left Charlotte abruptly, and she also knew the reasons why. Now it was rather juvenile of her to act as if she had no idea why Kate had left town. Obviously she just enjoyed jabbing at Kate, *or* she wanted to give Gary and Helen the impression that Kate's past was unsavory, to say the least. Probably, in Lydia's mind, that was true. But whatever her motivation was for this present cattiness, Kate wasn't prepared to cooperate by becoming visibly upset. Head held proud, she returned Lydia's stare.

"Yes, I guess you could say I left town abruptly."

"Oh, yes, indeed, I could say that and feel it was an understatement. What you actually did was run away, not surprising considering what you . . ."

"Lydia, this discussion is an absolute mystery to Helen and Gary. I suggest we drop it," Nathan intervened and his suggestion sounded much more like a firm command. Unobserved by anyone, he lightly squeezed Kate's shoulder before removing his arm from the back of the sofa to take one of his Lydia's hands in both his. "I'm sure you've had dinner but perhaps you'd like dessert here. Stella left a delicious strawberry torte."

Nathan's interruption of her building tirade had caused harsh resentful lines to mar Lydia's beautiful face, but she wisely didn't voice that resentment. The harsh lines vanished to be replaced by a facade of sophistication. She made a little moue with her mouth. "Ummm, strawberry torte. How you do tempt me, darling. You know that's my favorite but think of the billions of calories. I have to say no; I can't have any. Besides, since you've

142

obviously brought Gary and Miss Austin together here for a strictly business dinner, I don't want to intrude. I'll leave now, but I will definitely see you later, darling."

Rising with studied lazy grace after Nathan stood, Lydia immediately clasped her hands around his upper arm, exhibiting a proprietory air as she looked up at him through wide lushly lashed eyes. Finally, she turned her sweet smile on Gary and Helen. "You won't mind, will you, if I steal Nathan just for a minute to walk me to my car? All these surrounding trees make me a tad nervous, especially at night." After receiving their automatic assurances that they didn't mind, Lydia turned to Kate. "So nice to see you again, Miss Austin," she patently lied, something more than mere animosity suddenly glittering in her eyes. "Perhaps, this time, you'll stay in Charlotte longer than you did last time."

"Oh, I plan to. Who knows? I may work here in the main office until I'm old enough to retire," Kate replied blandly. "It's entirely possible. There are so many more career opportunities here. I can't imagine deciding to leave."

"Well, we'll see. Once a wanderer, always a wanderer, so they say. You might just pick up one day and be gone. Like the last time," Lydia said, a sharpness edging her drawling voice. She immediately dismissed Kate with a careless backward wave then cut her eyes up at Nathan. "Ready, darling?"

The two departed and Kate gave Helen and Gary a wan smile but was unable to speak. Upon Lydia's arrival, all the relaxed pleasure had gone out of the evening, and she couldn't shake the niggling feeling of despair that had come with seeing Nathan's former fiancée. Was he deeply involved with her again? Lydia's excessively possessive attitude toward him seemed to indicate he was. An intense aching jealousy created an emptiness within Kate. If Nathan did marry Lydia, what would *she* do? Run away again as she had run away six years ago from a hurt she couldn't cope with? No, not this time. This time, if it proved necessary, she would stay and face the pain. It would be agonizing to think

143

of Nathan and Lydia as man and wife but the agony would ease with time. Kate would survive. Feeling she had to prepare herself for the worst that could happen, she mentally assured herself that she was strong. Even if Nathan did marry Lydia, Kate knew she wouldn't wither up and die, although at that moment the mere thought made her imagine she might.

Nathan was outside with Lydia a long time. Every second that ticked by seemed more like a century, and as Kate nodded perfunctorily and responded absently whenever Helen or Gary spoke to her, her spirits sank lower and lower. Nathan wasn't one to neglect guests; the only reason he might do so was if he had something important to discuss with someone he cared a great deal about. Finally, Kate had to force from her mind the image of Nathan and Lydia outside together in the pale moonlight and, partially successful in that attempt, she was chatting amicably with the Roberts when Nathan at last walked back into the den.

Lydia's visit, however, had hastened the end of the evening. Helen and Gary's spirits seemed somewhat dampened also and only twenty or so minutes after Nathan's return, they announced they should be going. When they had left, Kate was alone once more with Nathan but rather than feeling excited as she had before dinner, she now felt both physically and emotionally weary. She needed time alone. It was only a few seconds after hearing Gary wheel his car out of the driveway that she got up from the love seat with a tentative motion of one hand.

"Dinner was excellent, Nathan. And I enjoyed the evening with Gary and Helen. And you," she said sincerely. "But I think I should go now too."

"What! And leave me with all those dishes?" Nathan protested, only half jokingly. "Oh, come on, Katie, surely you wouldn't do that to me?"

Kate couldn't help smiling. "You could make a fortune as a con artist," she told him but led the way into the kitchen nevertheless.

The automatic dishwasher made tidying the kitchen a quick and easy task. Less than fifteen minutes later, Kate was finishing the clean-up operation by removing the antique linen cloth from the oak table in the dining room. After folding it carefully, she gave it to Nathan, who laid it atop a stack of placemats on a lower shelf of the china cabinet. She watched him, her gaze riveted on the rippling of shoulder muscles that stretched taut the fabric of his shirt when he bent over to reach the back of the shelf. Because he had arrived home late and immediately started preparing dinner, he hadn't had time to change from the clothes he had worn to the office. He had shed the coat and vest of the charcoal gray suit and rolled the sleeves of his white shirt up to the elbows. Suddenly his rather rumpled appearance caused Kate's heart to catch, as she realized for the first time how very hectic his life was. Since his father's semiretirement, Nathan had taken over the running of the department store chain. Hundreds of employees depended on his executive skills for their very source of livelihood and that had to be an awesome weight of responsibility resting on his shoulders. It was a responsibility he was quite capable of bearing yet, watching him, Kate wondered if life at the top was lonely as she had always heard. When faced with difficult decisions or seemingly insoluble problems, did Nathan have anyone with whom he could discuss them, someone who was understanding and reassuring and could provide an oasis of peace amidst the frantically paced rat race of the business world? Recalling the faint lines of strain around his mouth and eyes that she had detected on occasion, Kate began to believe the unbelievable—Nathan Cordell, iron-willed and self-reliant as he was, still needed someone. And, in that instant of realization, she would have given anything, anything at all, to become the person he needed more than anyone else in the world.

Dangerous thoughts, futile hopes. She realized that any vulnerability in Nathan could make her even more susceptible to him than she already was. And the simple fact that he needed someone didn't mean she would be the one he chose to fill the empty space in his life. *Oh, if only he would choose her, though* . . . Kate closed her eyes. Her thoughts were taking a too fanciful turn, and she hastily untied the apron she had put back on to clear the dishes.

"Well, that's that. Everything's all nice and neat again," she said with forced cheeriness when Nathan turned away from the china cabinet toward her. She held out the apron. "I'll be going now. It's late and . . ."

"Not that late, Katie, not too late for this," he responded, taking the apron from her only to toss it atop the oak table. Long fingers encircled her small wrist; he stepped closer and pulled her to him, a hand sweeping down her back over her hips, molding the rounded contours of her woman's body to the virile lineation of his. They fit together so perfectly. Made for each other, made for each other ran repeatedly through Kate's mind, her thought processes becoming as erratic as her thundering heartbeat. When she lifted her head and he lowered his, their lips met, tactilely explored, then were forged together in the white hot flame of mutual need. Kate couldn't heed the warning signals ringing in her head; they grew fainter and fainter, soon to be silenced and forgotten completely. Later she might feel regret, but now innate caution and the fear of being hurt emotionally were powerless compared to her swiftly rising desire to be as close to Nathan as a woman can be to a man. Nothing mattered as much as being near him.

Perhaps gauging the depth of her response by the tremulous opening of her mouth to the demanding persuasive prowess of his, Nathan lifted her up in his arms and carried her upstairs. There the moonlight filtered through the leafy branches of the trees and shone through the French windows in dappled pools of opalescent illumination. Nathan lowered Kate's feet to the floor. Large hands spanned her waist and slipped upward, following the fitted bodice of her dress to the full upsweeping curves of her breasts. His fingers pressed into soft yet firmly resilient flesh, squeezing lightly and caressing; his palms stroked over invitingly warm peaks, playing teasingly and seducing until he could feel the tumescent nipples harden even through the fabric of both bra and dress. Her unconcealable response caused a shudder to run over him. His fingers pressed harder, but not completely ungently, into superbly structured rounded feminine flesh.

"Katie, *love,* I want you! You've been driving me crazy all week; Sunday was so long ago," he whispered hoarsely, lips firmly demanding surrender as they rubbed back and forth over the fuller softer shape of her own. As she moved closer, gazed up at him in the moonlight, and brushed exploring fingertips over the angular planes of his face, his hands roamed over the sides of her breasts around to her back where he sought the zipper of her dress. Lowering it with maddening slowness, he watched her face and the mesmerizing glint in his eyes reflected inner passion and an outward shimmer of moonlight. He slipped the dress off and her slip, then the remaining undergarments that were her last protective barrier to his wandering gaze.

He took one step back, his smile lazy as he surveyed the satin sheen of bare smooth skin. He reached out, weighed the fullness of her breasts in cupped hands. "You're always lovely, my Katie," he murmured, thumbs playing over hard roseate tips. "But never so lovely as you are like this, smooth and soft and deliciously naked."

Feeling drugged by the nearly wanton desires he had aroused, Kate moved into his arms with a low sound that was almost a whimper. "Oh, damn, Nathan," she moaned against the rising column of his neck. "Why can't I ever say no to you?"

The deep rumble of his muted laughter tingled in her ear. "Oh but you can say no. And often do. I'm just delighted you don't want to say no tonight. Do you?"

Kate staged a last-ditch battle against rising need. "I should say no," she breathed. "I shouldn't let this happen; I shouldn't stay here. If Lydia comes back . . ."

"Lydia won't be back, claims she's afraid to drive alone in this

147

remote area at night. You needn't worry about her." Outlining her lips with one fingertip, he covered the gentle sloping of her shoulders with light nibbling kisses. "And although you think you should say no, you aren't going to this time, are you, Katie?"

Kate made a low soft sound again and trembled. Those tiny nipping kisses were driving her wild. She closed her eyes and swayed slightly, weakened by the sudden intense dizzying of her senses. When, to steady her, Nathan's hands encircled her bare waist, the hot ache of longing engulfed her, swept away the last fragments of her will to resist, and she opened her eyes partially. Gazing up at him beneath the thick fringe of her lashes, she signaled both mental and physical surrender with a quavering sigh.

"Oh, Nathan, you always win," she softly accused, even as she sought the buttons of his shirt with shaky fingers. Undoing them, she smiled resignedly. "Somehow, you just always win."

"Not always. Not nearly often enough, in my opinion," he disagreed softly, watching as she tugged his shirttail from beneath the waistband of his trousers. "But right now, none of that matters anyway. All that matters is tonight and how we're going to spend it. Becoming a part of each other. Isn't that the way it is with us, Katie?"

She nodded. That was exactly the way it was, except that she had thought that she alone experienced that aspect of their lovemaking. Now, knowing he also sensed to some degree at least that incredible bond between them when they made love, she was freed of the regret she had felt because her need to surrender completely to him had overruled strength of will. If he too felt even a little of that wondrous sense of belonging, she was willing to give everything of herself.

Pausing in the removal of his shirt, she drew her hands in slow circular motions down his chest to just beneath his ribs, feathering them along his lean sides and round beneath his shirt to his broad back. She heard the tenor of his breathing quicken and smiled secretively when he impatiently stripped off his shirt himself. A rushing thrill made her own breath catch when he gripped her arms, lifting her close against him while his mouth descended on hers, insistently parting her lips. She yielded totally, her warm body acquiescent. Shivers of sensations ran over her skin as he explored the creamy smoothness of her arched back inch by inch. Her fingers tangled in his hair until he dragged her hands down to the buckle of his belt. Unwilling to move away from him long enough to undo it, she shook her head and, with her arms still around him, moved back slightly, toward the bed.

"No, not here. Outside, on the deck," he said roughly, reaching around her to pull the quilted coverlet from his bed. Draping it over one arm while his other slipped around her waist, he held her close to his side and started toward the opened French windows. Kate hesitated and he stopped for an instant. Tilting her head back, she looked up at him, detecting a swift smile of tender amusement. "Yes, outside, Katie," he repeated softly, leaning down to place a kiss on the tip of her nose. "We've never made love outside before, a lack we'll make up for tonight."

"But . . ."

"It's a very private place. You know that. Think of the trees surrounding us," he whispered, moving her forward again. "Come on, Katie, don't be shy."

Yet, she did feel shy, amazingly shy, as he led her out onto the deck in the moonlight. A gentle breeze caressed her skin, intensifying her feeling of vulnerability, but Nathan gave her no chance to demure a second time. He kissed her with a deliberately controlled passion that was somehow reassuring. Letting her go for a moment, he spread the quilted coverlet over the vinyl cushions of a wide chaise lounge. He lowered the backrest until the bed beneath the trees was perfectly flat, then turned back to Kate. He extended his hands, his intent gaze never leaving her face as her fingertips grazed his palms when she put her hands in his. He drew her to him, kissed her again, then picked her up and lowered her onto the lounge, sitting down on the edge to sweep shadowed eyes over the entire length of her body, just

149

visible in the moonlight. Masculinely rough fingertips touched her chin before he got up again.

Kate's eyes followed as he strode across the deck to the round table where they had enjoyed the quiet, impromptu Sunday dinner. When he returned to her, he carried a tapered candle encircled by a clear glass lamp chimney. With a lighter from his pocket, he lit the candle and placed it on a smaller table some feet distance. Soft amber light fell over Kate and him, but she was so absorbed in the bronzed glow of his bare torso in the candle's mellow illumination that she forgot for a moment about her own nakedness.

Nathan didn't. In the shadow of an overhanging eave, he shed the remainder of his clothing then came out of the darkness to her. He towered over her, looking down at her appealingly small face framed by the glorious thickness of her hair. Kate looked back up at him until she felt oddly as if he were assimilating her entire being into his. She closed her eyes, felt the cushion yield to his weight as he sat down beside her, and trembled almost unnoticeably when his bare skin brushed her bare thigh.

But Nathan noticed and murmured, "Cold, Katie?"

"Not . . . cold really," she answered. "But a little cool."

"Not for long," he promised then laughed softly when her eyes flew open and she stared up at him. Stretching out beside her, he turned her toward him, still smiling while laying a hand on her waist. "Katie, Katie, how can you still be shy with me after all the hours we've spent together like this?"

Maybe it's because I know you don't love me, Kate replied longingly but not in spoken words. That was the reason for any shyness she still felt with him, but she couldn't tell him that. She said nothing instead, unwilling to reveal all too clearly her feelings for him.

"Luckily, there's a woman with fiery passions beneath that sometimes shy exterior," he said, breaking the silence between them. "And that's the woman you'll be tonight."

His arm glided around her; he moved to kiss her, but Kate

couldn't let it be so very easy for him. Putting a hand between them, against his chest, she voiced the relentless nagging suspicion that had been growing in her mind since he had led her out here. "Nathan, have there been—" she began, halted, then started again—"have you made love to other women out here?"

Nathan's tenderly amused smile disappeared. The swift sobering of his expression accompanied the narrowing of his level gaze. He shook his head. "Never. I'd never even thought about bringing any woman out here until tonight."

Kate nibbled her lower lip. "You're sure?"

"I think I would remember if I'd ever made love to anyone out here," he retorted wryly. "But why is it so important for you to know that? You almost sound jealous."

"Just proud," she lied, unable to look directly at him. "I really wouldn't want to be known as 'number whatever on the chaise lounge.'"

"Umm, I see. But you are a number, Katie. One. The only one. Believe me?"

If he was trying to seduce her with words, he was having some success. Now Kate couldn't look away from him and was searching his face for some sign of duplicity, but nothing about his straightforward gaze indicated he could be lying. She breathed deeply. "I guess I'll just have to take your word for it, won't I?"

"I guess you will. Unless you want a signed affadavit from every woman I know or have ever known since I moved here?"

Kate was unable to suppress an answering smile. "Not a very practical idea, considering all the women you know. It might take forever just to round up all of them."

Nathan made no reply and soon a hushed silence wrapped around them, seeming to enclose them in their own very exclusive little world. He moved his head, seeking the corners of her mouth tugged upward by her smile, kissing first one, then the other, again and again until the breathless parting of her lips was as uncontrollable as the quickening of her heartbeat. Moving with lissome grace, Kate was closer to him, one arm draping across his shoulders while his tightened around her waist. The tip of his tongue explored the opening flower of her mouth, tasting sweetness, setting off tingling sensations as he probed the full curving of her lips. Each successive kiss they exchanged lengthened until every one seemed almost an intimate act in itself. Kate felt exhilaratingly alive. Her senses responded with fantastic keenness to every stimuli: Nathan's warm minty breath, the faint fragrance of lime after-shave, the enticingly male texture of hair-roughened skin. Her eyes opened to adore the look of him; his whispered endearments became all she ever wanted to hear. And her fascination with him was heightened by his fascination with her.

His mouth took hers again and again, as if he could never get his fill of the sweetness of her lips although she offered all of herself as she eagerly returned his kisses.

"You smell delicious. You taste delicious," he whispered huskily, nibbling the tender lobe of one ear. He moved his head slightly to look into her eyes and unbridled passion flared in the depths of his. "God, I could devour you. My sweet Katie."

And she was his, lost in him, knowing nothing except her rising need of him. And he had been right. She no longer felt the least bit chilled. The touch of his hands sweeping over the graceful lines of her body heated her skin and ignited an inner blaze that burned in a central shaft of fire deep within her. Aroused as only he could arouse her, she ached for much more than feathering caresses and kisses that tantalized. And the intimate exploration that followed only stoked the raging fire inside her. Her breathing swift and shallow as his, she clung to him, kissing him with all the passion in her, seeking to unleash the power of his hot desire.

She succeeded. With a groan muffled against her lips, Nathan moved her beneath him, his strong lean body holding her captive. He slipped a hand between satiny shapely thighs, parting them, lowering himself between them. As Kate's eyes slowly opened, the blue glint in his impaled them, held them with hypnotizing intensity.

"*Love me,*" Kate found herself whispering. "Nathan, love me now.".

"Oh, I intend to. And now, sweet Katie. Right now," he whispered back and with a thrust that was both gentle and demanding, he entered a secret warmth that yielded with exquisite receptiveness to potently aroused masculinity.

Kate's soft gasp of pleasure accompanied the complete merging of their bodies. Feeling that special bond again, that feeling of oneness with him, she arched upward, wrapping herself closer and closer to him. He moved slowly at first, almost teasingly, but she moved with him, luxuriating in the steadily heightening pleasure they were sharing. She opened her eyes, looking up at the moonlight filtering through the leaves, then at Nathan's dark face above her. Touching her hair, he smiled lazily at her and she smiled back, loving him so much in that poignant moment that she might have told him if he hadn't gently kissed her again, silencing the words before she had any chance to voice them.

Bathed in the candlelight and the leaf-filtered beams of the moon moving across the black velvet sky above them, they experienced delights together Kate had never really believed existed. Intuitively, she knew that with anyone other than Nathan she would never have known such pleasures; with him, she gloried in them. Love made the difference. And even if only she loved and he couldn't love her in return, for tonight at least, her happiness came with the giving of herself. Brushing her lips into the hollow at the base of his throat, she murmured his name over and over, love deepening her voice to a throaty huskiness.

Much later, when they were lifted up together to the exquisite peak of rapture, then, together, drifted down into the hazy warmth of complete fulfillment, Kate snuggled as close to Nathan as she could, content in the tender aftermath. She smiled as he stroked her hair back from her face, but when his hand moved down her back, his fingertips drifting over the delicately boned length of her spine, she trembled.

"We'll go inside," Nathan said softly. "The breeze is cool."

When he got up to wrap her snugly in the quilted coverlet then picked her up with little effort in strong arms to carry her into his room, she could have told him that the cold air hadn't made her tremble. It had been his feathery touch on her back that induced the tremor as it brought back in an instant the awesome power of all the sweetly piercing sensations she had just experienced with him. But she said nothing. His bundling her up to take her inside was such an endearingly tender gesture that she didn't want to tamper with it. If he wished to protect her from the cold, she was more than willing to be protected by him.

After brushing a kiss against her neck, she smiled drowsily up at him as he carried her to his bed. He pulled back the top sheet and laid her down to unwind the coverlet around her and draw it from beneath her. Then he was beside her, reaching over to switch off the bedside lamp before tucking the quilted covering tightly around both of them. A lean finger lifted Kate's chin. Nathan kissed her, and almost before her head settled comfortably in the hollow of his shoulder, she slept.

Kate awoke early. She stretched with the lazy fluidity of a contented kitten until she suddenly realized last night had been real, not a dream. Her heart immediately began a heavier beat that thudded thickly in her ears. She turned her face into her pillow, muffling the strained mournful sound she made. The night was over; morning had come and in the clearer light of a new day, she was afraid again. *What was wrong with her?* How had she been so weak-willed last night that she had let Nathan use her again? Why did she go on surrendering to him and her own need again and again, giving more and more of herself each time, until now her love for him was deeper than it had ever been? Those questions chased each other around in circles in her tired brain, but she could find no answer to any of them.

She didn't know why she did anything anymore, and that was more than frightening. It was terrifying. Hot tears filled her eyes. Giving in to Nathan time and again could only cause her agonizing grief. Once, six years ago, she had lost him and had been able to convince herself that she had never truly loved him anyhow, but it wouldn't be possible for her to do that ever again. This time when he finished with her, she wouldn't be able to tell herself lies. A girl's love had become a woman's and too deeply ingrained in her to be denied. Yet, even if she did have to face living forever in the shadow of an unrequited love, she certainly didn't have to torture herself like this. Every night she spent with him could only intensify the pain she would eventually have to deal with. And it was sheer madness to go on this way, accepting whatever tenderness he wanted to give her in return for the very essence of her being. *Insanity!* That's what it was, and she had to find a cure before she lost the little bit of control she still had over her own existence.

Was this, however, one of those times when the cure was as painful as the malady? Kate knew it must be because the only way to cut her losses was to never allow herself to be close to Nathan again, and simply the thought of that caused her excruciating pain. Fresh tears filled her eyes, blurring her vision and spilling over onto her cheeks, and when she heard Nathan entered the bedroom, she barely had time to wipe them away before he could see them.

Obviously, she did a poor job of it. The moment Nathan stepped up to the bed, and she forced herself to turn over and look at him, a quick frown furrowed his brow. He was carrying two cups of coffee on a tray but deposited that on the table before sitting down on the edge of the bed.

"Tears, Katie?" he muttered, his fingers not particularly gentle as he brushed away the traitorous teardrop that had caught in the feathery fringe of her lower lashes and brought itself to his attention with the sparkle of a tiny crystal. As Nathan brought his hand back away from Kate's unusually pale face, his own features were drawn to a finely honed hardness. His eyes were icy green chips, and there was neither sympathy nor any real concern in his stony expression. "Why? What the hell do you have to cry about?"

Blinking back the unshed tears that still ached to be released, Kate gestured uncertainly. "I don't know why but I just started to cry."

"You're lying," he stated bluntly. "Now, how about the truth, Katie?"

Kate sniffled. "It's just that . . . well, when I woke up, remembering what happened last night . . . Oh, Nathan, this is all so crazy. I shouldn't have stayed here with you. Then I wanted to stay, but now I know I just can't cope with this kind of relation . . ."

"Don't bother to say anymore," he interrupted grimly, rising beside her, hands balled into fists and thrust deep into his robe's pockets. "I don't want to hear another word of it. Believe it or not, I've finally lost all patience. Lydia was right about you. You do love to run away. Run then. It's getting late anyhow. You'd better rush to the hotel and change clothes before you go to the office." With a derisive twist of his lips, he turned away and strode toward the door. One hand on the handle, he looked back. "You now have my permission to wallow in your guilt about Phillip's death to your heart's content. I hope you enjoy every minute of it, Kate."

Kate. No longer Katie which had always sounded like an endearment the way he said it. But now, she was Kate to him, as if the little affection he had felt for her had disappeared completely. Trembling, Kate sat up in bed, staring at the door he had closed with unnecessary force on his way out. A thick, almost strangling constriction twisted painfully in her chest. He had totally misunderstood her feelings. But perhaps it was better

156

this way. The sooner it ended, the quicker the healing process could begin.

"Better *this* way?" Kate said aloud, her voice catching on a half sob as she got out of Nathan's bed. If it was better this way, why did she feel so damned bad? Why was an aching void spreading within her? Why, if it was better this way, did her life seem to stretch out before her bleak and empty and horribly lonely?

CHAPTER NINE

Kate didn't like living in the hotel. As Nathan had predicted, she was beginning to find even the rather spacious suite confining. She wanted a place of her own where she would be surrounded by her own belongings, and most of all, she wanted a kitchen. Though she had never aspired to becoming a gourmet chef, she did like to dabble with new recipes and prepare her own meals most of the time rather than constantly eating in restaurants as she was forced to do while at the hotel. Of course there was room service which she began to call with increasing frequency as her stay was prolonged but eating in her suite couldn't compare with preparing her own meals in a place she could call home.

Around ten o'clock on the Thursday evening after she had spent the night with Nathan, Kate glanced around the sitting room of her suite. She couldn't deny its lovely decor, but there was something so innately sterile about living in a hotel that she could no longer really appreciate the suite's surface beauty. With a resigned sigh, she went into the adjoining bedroom, deciding she might as well go to bed. She certainly preferred sleeping to staying up and being bored to tears. After slipping out of her jeans and shirt and into a cool cotton nightgown, Kate sat down at the vanity and brushed her hair with brisk even strokes until her hand suddenly paused midair. Gazing at her reflection in the mirror, she recalled the weekend just past. She had returned to Raleigh to retrieve her car and to supervise the first step in the transfer of her belongings to a storage warehouse here in Charlotte. As the movers were loading the last box onto their van, Joe had arrived at the apartment building because she had called and asked him to meet her there. Since Nathan had come back into her life, Joe hardly ever entered her mind, and she felt she owed it to him to tell him in person that their relationship had ended. He had not taken the news well and stubbornly insisted they still plan to visit each other on weekends. When she had assured him that visits back and forth between them couldn't alter her feelings, he had accused her of being involved with Nathan, an accusation she had neither denied nor confirmed. Furious, Joe had left her, but Kate hadn't regretted making the break between them both permanent and swift. That way was kinder. She wouldn't have wanted to keep him dangling on a string, hoping to someday receive from her an emotional commitment she would never be capable of giving to anyone except Nathan.

This past weekend then, she had burned all her bridges behind her. After Kate brushed her teeth, when she was getting into bed, she smiled rather bitterly. Yes, she had burned her bridges and for what? For Nathan, who since this morning had only twice spoken to her, and both those times had been so cold and indifferent that it seemed he didn't remember there had ever been any closeness between them. His attitude hurt Kate badly, but to escape the pain, she threw herself into her office duties, deliberately driving herself to the point of exhaustion, so she wouldn't have to deal with the agony of insomnia too.

Tonight, bone-weary, she curled up in a self-protective ball in her bed, hugged her pillow to her, and soon fell into a troubled sleep. Dreams about Nathan plagued her but that was not unusual. It was when she drifted into a dream with vaguely menacing overtones that she awoke with a start and froze in her bed. Then she heard it, a distinct scraping sound outside the bedroom door that opened into the corridor. She held her breath and her eyes widened when that sound was followed by another, the muted grinding of the doorknob being turned slowly back and forth. Kate pressed a fist between her breasts, trying to believe she wasn't fully awake and still in the grip of her last menacing dream. But when the scraping noise came again, and she recalled Nathan's warning about a jewel thief, her heart seemed to leap far up in her throat.

Quietly as possible, she called the desk, told the clerk in a whisper what she was hearing, then replaced the receiver silently in its cradle. Though it actually took less than a minute for help to arrive, it seemed much longer than that to Kate. And when she heard the desk clerk's voice outside her door, she flew from bed, slipping into her robe on the run as she rushed to let him in. With him were the night manager, a bellman, and the hotel security chief, who examined the door while the other men filed into the room.

With supreme effort, Kate arranged her face into composed lines and kept her voice steady as she related all she had heard yet by the time she finished, she was still unable to stop her hands from trembling. To hide them, she clasped them tightly together behind her back.

"Well, looks like somebody did try to get in," the security chief announced rather casually. "See these scratches around the lock here?"

After peering closely, the night manager dismissed them with the toss of a hand. "Probably just another guest who thought this was his room and kept trying to unlock it until he realized his mistake," he told Kate hastily. "I can almost assure you that's what happened, Miss Austin. Of course, we'll check the stairwells anyway to be sure no one's around who shouldn't be. Okay?"

She nodded, eager to believe his fairly plausible explanation. Yet, after she had convinced the men that she was perfectly calm once more and they had gone away, she left a lamp on in the room and went back to bed but with sincere doubts that she would fall asleep easily again.

She was right. Half an hour later, she was still wide awake, lying tensed in bed, staring up at the ceiling, ears attuned to every little sound, real or imagined. Alert as she was, however, she nearly jumped out of her skin when someone suddenly tapped softly on her door. She got out of bed. Her heart pounded and she trembled as she tiptoed across the room while slipping on her robe. She stopped to nervously nibble a fingernail before calling out, "Who . . . who is it?"

"Nathan," his deep voice came back. "Open the door, Katie."

As relief washed over her, she did so eagerly, never so glad to see anyone in her life as she was to see him standing in the hallway. In khaki pants and a cream polo shirt, he raked his fingers through rumpled hair, and it was obvious he had come straight from bed.

"The night manager says you had quite a scare," he explained his presence while walking past her into the room. "He said you were still shaking when he and the others left you and decided to call me. Since the store's putting you up here, you're my responsibility."

Kate almost winced. His *responsibility*. How cold and impersonal that sounded. And insulting. If he had only come because he felt *responsible* for her for purely business reasons, she wished he had just stayed in bed. Her expression became defensively cool. "I appreciate your coming, but I'm fine now. The manager shouldn't have bothered you because you're *not* responsible for me. And you've lost sleep for nothing if that's why you came."

"Oh, hell, Katie, I don't know why I'm here," he muttered, raking fingers through his hair again. "You're right. I didn't have to come but something made me. I guess I just didn't like to think of you alone here and scared."

"You still shouldn't have bothered." Still on the defensive, she shrugged carelessly. "I got scared for no good reason, probably.

161

Maybe it was just another guest mistaking my room for his. But I remembered what you'd told me about the jewel thief hitting hotels around here and panicked a little, I guess."

"But, for God's sake, Katie, I . . ." His words halted abruptly then he shrugged and looked piercingly into her soft green eyes. "You weren't asleep when I knocked just now, were you?" When she shook her head honestly, he gestured toward the closet. "Get a suitcase and pack a few things. I'll take you to my house tonight, and tomorrow you can come get the rest of your belongings and check out of here. Until you find an apartment, you'll stay with me."

"Nathan, you know I can't do that," she protested, though for a second she wished desperately that she could go home with him. "People would talk if I stayed with you, and besides, I've put a deposit on an apartment. I can't move in for two more weeks because the present tenants aren't leaving until then, but I can stand it here that long. I just can't stay with you for over two weeks."

He shrugged as if he couldn't have cared less. "Suit yourself then. If you want to lie awake all night every night for the next two weeks, hearing every little sound, imagining the jewel thief's trying to break in, be my guest. Seems foolish to me but the choice is yours."

"Nathan, wait, please," Katie said softly as he turned and started to walk away. His mention of the jewel thief had brought too clearly to mind the scraping sound that had awakened her earlier and uneasiness crept over her again. Nathan had stopped and was regarding her questioningly. She lifted one hand, almost as if to reach out to him but allowed it to drop again instead and murmured, "I'm still a little nervous about what happened tonight. Do you think you could . . . I mean, would you stay here for a little while with me? I hate to ask but . . ."

"Katie, you little idiot, come here," he said roughly, pulling her close against his long lean body and immediately feeling the trembling that shook her slight frame. "Don't be scared. It prob-

162

ably *was* another guest thinking this was his room. Try not to tremble so; everything's all right now."

Lulled by softly murmured reassurances and gentle stroking hands on her back, Kate did begin to relax. She curled up cozily in Nathan's lap when he picked her up and sat down in the stuffed chair beside her bed, but it was only a few minutes later when his comforting touch started to become more sensuously caressing. Kate tensed, knowing what was happening and desperate to stop it before it was too late. She had promised herself she would never let him make love to her again! But when she tried to move out of his arms and off his lap, his hold on her tightened, preventing her escape as his mouth sought and found hers. His hard lips exerted a slight twisting pressure, possessing the softness of hers, and she knew at once he didn't intend to let her go. His hands roved over her, urgently following every curve and contouring line, and when he dragged off her robe then her thin nightgown, nearly ripping that garment in his haste to unclothe her, his overwhelming passion caught her up in its grip. Excitement coursed through her and was built to an electrifyingly intense peak by the touch of his hands and his mouth and the hard body she was molded so close to.

It had never been quite this way between them. Always before, Nathan had slowly seduced Kate, then held rein on his own desire, only satisfying his needs after satisfying hers. She thought she had known the depth of his passion in those moments when he had taken his pleasure, but now she was understanding for the first time what unleashed passion was really like. Nathan's fierce kisses were demanding total surrender while he explored every inch of her, his touch branding on her skin a right of possession she knew instinctively he would have taken by force had she tried to withhold it. As it was, she didn't. She was powerless to fight him. Passion had become a raging tempest, beyond the control of either of them, and Kate was swept up with him in a maelstrom of swirling need.

Nathan took her to bed and brought her hands to his belt,

compelling her to unbuckle it while he bent over her, his mouth closing around the tip of first one throbbing breast, then the other. His tongue rubbing over the ruched nipples sent such shockwaves of incredible delight rushing through her that she was hardly aware that he had shed his trousers until his mouth released her breasts when he straightened to pull his polo shirt off over his head. Naked, he moved over her, supporting most of his weight on his elbows as he slipped her small fingers between his to bring her hands up above her head on the pillow. A muscle ticked in his rock hard jaw as he looked down at her face, and there was unmistakable intent in his darkened eyes.

"Mine, Katie, you *are* mine," he said through clenched teeth. "Aren't you?"

"Yes, Nathan," she breathed. "Only yours."

He whispered her name in triumph when a muffled cry of delight escaped her lips with the swift penetrating union of their bodies. He released her hands, and when she wrapped her arms around his waist, he kissed her, whispering into her mouth, "Yes, Katie, mine. No one else can have you."

He took her with an intensity she had never known in him before, and she responded in kind, giving joyously and taking from him. Though the very depth of his unrestrained passion made him less gentle than usual, he never sought to hurt or humiliate or abuse her. He gave as much pleasure as he took and transported her with him up to the highest spires of sensation and over into delicious fulfillment.

"No tears this time, Katie?" he murmured later as they lay wrapped in each other's arms. "Aren't you going to cry because you're ashamed of what we have together?"

"No, because I'm not ashamed," she answered because she wasn't. She was simply afraid. Yet, she had realized tonight that even her fear of emotional pain seemed weak and puny compared with her need to be close to him. Eventually she was going to have to regain control of her response to him, but at that moment she didn't want to think about self-control or rather her obvious lack of it. She simply wanted to float on with Nathan on this soft cloud of mutual contentment.

"If you don't feel ashamed then why won't you just go home with me?" Nathan continued as she snuggled closer to him. "It's the only sensible thing to do. You don't want to stay here and feel frightened for over two weeks, do you?"

"No, but . . . I still think it would be very unwise to stay with you."

"Why? Because people might start gossiping about us?"

"No, it's not . . . that *exactly.*"

"Then what is it *exactly*?"

"I don't know," she lied. "It just seems unwise."

"You see. You just admitted there's no logical reason you shouldn't stay with me," he whispered, his breath tickling her ear. He drew her tight against him and, with an incredibly gentle hand, smoothed her hair. "Katie, why must you always resist? Give in to what you want, what I want. And I want you to come stay with me."

"But . . ."

"You can't think it's better for us to go on with these 'one night stands'?" he persisted cajolingly, tenderly massaging her bare back. "A night at my house, a night here at your hotel—that really is an arrangement the gossips could have a ball with. You know that, don't you?"

Kate's resolve was wavering, and she was well aware of that fact. His coaxing voice and expertly caressing hands were beginning to melt away the core of her deep-seated need to protect herself. And vulnerable as she was feeling in the afterglow of their lovemaking, she was afraid that if he really put his mind to it, he might be able to convince her to do anything he wished. Wise enough to be scared of her own susceptibility, she sought an indefinite postponement of their discussion.

"Ummm, I just can't think straight right now," she sighed, nuzzling her head against his shoulder, willing to resort to feminine wiliness in this dangerous situation. She rubbed soft lips over smooth skin. "Couldn't we talk about all this later? I'm so sleepy, Nathan."

"We'll talk tomorrow then," he stated firmly, arms tightening around her. "But if you're trying to play for time, Kate, it won't work. Tomorrow, I'll still expect you to decide to come stay with me."

"Ummm," was Kate's response as she pretended she was nearly asleep. But long after Nathan's breathing became slower and perfectly measured, she lay awake.

What would it be like to live in Nathan's secluded home with him? How would it be to wake up every morning and find him beside her in bed? It would be heavenly; that's how it would be. And that realization frightened her more than anything else. Staying with Nathan for two weeks only to have to leave and be alone again would be like having a glimpse of paradise then being forbidden to ever have another glimpse. Since Nathan had reentered her life, Kate had gambled more recklessly than she had ever imagined she could, but what he was asking her to do now involved far too much risk. She didn't want to live her life, knowing what true happiness was yet never being able to attain it again. That would be a tragedy, and she had no wish to become a tragic figure, a spinster with only a cat to talk to and only the memory of two happy weeks to warm the lonely nights.

Besides, there was really no guarantee that the two weeks with him would be perfectly idyllic. Because, by agreeing to stay with him, she had become a challenge conquered and an objective achieved, he might very well be bored with her before the two weeks ended. And if that didn't happen, there was Lydia to consider. If she discovered Kate was living at Nathan's, she might try to do everything in her power to put a stop to that arrangement and that would add yet another complication to the situation.

Yes, going to stay with Nathan would be a risk Kate was either too cowardly or too wise to take. During the past several weeks, she had become a gambler, but she was not a fool. She could still recognize a no-win situation, and this was one. Drawing in a long tremulous breath then slowly releasing it, Kate slipped her hand across Nathan's chest and moved as close to him as she could. Tomorrow wasn't going to be easy. Giving up even the most foolish last hope never is. And Kate would be giving up every hope of having any kind of personal relationship with Nathan when she told him tomorrow that she couldn't move from the hotel to his house. She knew she would be. He had already said he had no more patience. After she told him her decision tomorrow, he would be through with her.

Agonizing as that prospect was, Kate knew she would do what she had to do. She needed much longer than two weeks of happiness with Nathan, and she needed for him to feel more for her than a strong physical attraction. She needed his love. But if he didn't love her now, he never would, and it would be self-destructive to continue hoping for what she couldn't have, like a child crying for the moon. Tears of regret stung Kate's eyes, but a slender, tempered core of steely inner strength prevented her from shedding them. She might cry a great deal later, but she wouldn't cry now. She had probably just made the most important decision in her life, but it would be foolish to cry because the decision she had made was the right one.

CHAPTER TEN

"Oh yes, it was definitely the right decision," Kate whispered to herself. Her jaw tight, she stared across the chest-high clipped hedge that meandered through the park, transfixed by the sight of Nathan's arm across Lydia Plemmons' shoulders as they sat kissing on a park bench. Kate pressed trembling fingers to her lips. She had walked by and glanced across the hedge just in time to see Lydia initiate the kiss, but she could also see that Nathan was making no effort to put a quick end to it. As Kate stood watching, the kiss seemed to go on forever, and even after Nathan and Lydia finally separated, the tender smile he gave the other woman sent a stiletto-sharp pain tearing through her chest. She had been stunned at first; now, she was hurting. Badly. Half blinded by tears, she swiftly turned around and proceeded back along the path in the direction from which she had come earlier.

With an impatient swipe of one hand, Kate brushed away the teardrops that were clinging to her lashes and resolutely staunched the flow of others that tried to follow with a grim tightening of her lips. Why in God's name had she picked today to wander through the park? Usually she took the main path through it when going for lunch and when returning to the office.

Today, however, her appetite had been practically nonexistent and, unwilling to sit staring at her food for nearly an hour, she had decided a stroll in the park might help ease her dread of telling Nathan her decision. His secretary had called down to tell her he wanted to see her at three that afternoon, but Kate wasn't sure she could bear to keep that appointment now. If only she hadn't lingered so long in the park . . . Seeing Lydia with Nathan had been pure happenstance, sheer rotten luck, and the fact that seeing them together confirmed that last night's decision had been correct was certainly cold comfort to Kate. This was one of those times when she would have much preferred to have been proven wrong.

It simply hadn't worked out that way. Trying to accept the reality of the situation, Kate squared her shoulders as she automatically found her way out of the park. On the corner while she waited for the light to change, so she could cross the street, she could feel the dull thudding of her heart. She felt suddenly light-headed and weak and reached out for a street signpost to steady herself. She knew she really shouldn't have been shocked by seeing Nathan with Lydia. She had agonized often enough over the possibility that he was seriously involved with his ex-fiancée again. Yet in the park Kate had been deeply shocked because she had had some very basic feeling that he was not a man who could be callous enough to be deeply involved with two women at one time. A lot she had known. The scene in the park had certainly proved how wrong she had been and that caused her pain too. She had believed herself a better judge of character than that yet perhaps her love for Nathan had robbed her of all objectivity.

Feeling somewhat steadier now, Kate sighed heavily but dropped her hand from the signpost. That wonderfully amazing part of the brain that makes the body function normally even when the rest of the mind is in turmoil enabled her to get across the street, down half a block, and into the store again. Kate pushed the correct button inside the elevator and got off on the right floor, despite the fact she was barely aware of her surroundings. Head lowered, she walked slowly down the corridor toward her office. It suddenly occurred to her that she could leave Charlotte by asking to be transferred back to Raleigh. There, at least, she wouldn't have to face seeing Nathan every day and constantly reminded of his relationship with Lydia. *Back to Raleigh* . . . But no! Kate shook her head. Transferring to Raleigh would be running away, which Lydia had snidely predicted she would do, and Kate decided she would rather go through the fires of hell than to give Lydia the satisfaction of being right. She was going to remain in Charlotte and survive whatever had to be faced. If Nathan married Lydia, she would live. If together they had babies that all looked exactly like him, she would hide the pain she felt and survive.

The Kate she had been six years ago had cowardly run away, but she was different now and that was a positive thought to hang onto as she tried to cope with the dreadful sense of loss she felt. Deep in thought, her head still lowered, Kate continued along the hallway. When a door ahead of her suddenly opened, she didn't notice and walked headlong into Gary Roberts as he was leaving his office.

"Oh dear, I'm sorry, Gary," she apologized, smiling wanly at him. "I didn't see you coming out. Guess I'm a little preoccupied today."

"You're not sick, are you? You look pretty pale," Gary said, carefully examining her face. He took her arm. "And you're trembling! I think you'd better sit down a minute. Come in here."

Despite Kate's protest, she was led into the office of Gary's secretary who wasn't at her desk, apparently on lunch break. Deciding aquiescence was easier than arguing, Kate allowed Gary to seat her in a large overstuffed chair pushed back against one wall. She sank down in the thick cushion, wishing she had made it to her own office before Gary had seen her.

"Are you sick?" he asked again, sitting on the edge of his

secretary's desk. When Kate shook her head, he frowned. "What's wrong then? It's obvious something is. You are pale."

"I am a bit upset. Just a little personal problem. I'll be okay."

"I'd be happy to listen if it would help you to talk about it."

Kate smiled as perkily at him as she could. "I can tell you this much. I was just considering asking for a transfer back to Raleigh but . . ."

"You can't be serious?" Gary exclaimed. "Why do you want to transfer back there when you're just getting settled here?"

"I said I considered asking for a transfer, but I changed my mind," Kate explained, warmed by Gary's concern for her. "I'm not leaving Charlotte. No matter how much I might want to leave sometimes, I'm going to stay."

Gary's frown deepened. "Forgive me if I'm out of line here, but does all this have something to do with Nathan and Lydia Plemmons? I mean, Helen and I did notice that night at Nathan's that you became very quiet and a little pale then, too, when he walked Lydia to her car."

"Yes, I thought you'd both noticed that." With a humorless smile, Kate rose from the chair and glanced at her wristwatch. "I really can't explain right now. But it's nothing for you to worry about. I promise you I'm okay. And I should get to my office. It's going to be a busy afternoon."

"If you change your mind and need to talk, I'll be here," Gary said as she went to the doorway. "And I'm a very good listener."

Strangely close to tears again, Kate could only nod and return Gary's fond smile before she stepped into the hallway and headed for the sanctuary of her own little office.

Ninety minutes later, Kate had managed to lose herself in her work and was rushing downstairs to find Sue Latham, the head buyer for the entire chain of Cordell stores. Sue's assistant had given notice two days ago, and Kate needed to know if Sue had anyone in mind as a replacement. Sue was out of her office, supposedly in lingerie. Katie hurriedly threaded her way through racks and displays of very expensive sportswear, heading toward lingerie and suddenly stopped short when hailed by a vaguely familiar voice.

"*Katie!* Katie Austin. It *is* you! Someone told me you were working here again, but I didn't really think it could be true. But it is!"

As Kate turned toward the woman who was rapidly approaching, a delighted smile brightened her rather drawn features. "Janet Malone! Oh, it's so good to see you! When I got back to Charlotte, I hoped to find you listed in the phone directory. But you weren't and I assumed you had either moved or gotten married."

"Married. It's Janet Rawlins now."

The two young women hugged briefly, moved apart to inspect each other carefully, both smiling with excitement at this unexpected encounter.

"You look just fabulous," Kate declared. "Marriage obviously agrees with you."

"Umm, yes. Bill has to be the greatest husband in the world. Of course I might be a little prejudiced," Janet admitted, laughing when Kate did. Then she looked her old friend over carefully again. "You've hardly changed at all in six years, except maybe you're a little thinner. You really look terrific. Now tell me what you're doing here in Cordell's again." She nodded as Kate described her duties as assistant director of personnel, then a speculative gleam came into her soft brown eyes, and she leaned nearer to Kate to whisper, "Does this mean what I hope it does—that you and Nathan are back together again?"

The question was not too personal. When the two young women had clerked together at Cordell's six years ago, they had shared each other's secrets. Janet had known about the beginnings of Kate's involvement with Nathan, though she had never learned how far that involvement progressed the night Phillip had died because Kate had been unable to face returning to Charlotte after that tragic weekend. Now it seemed in a way as

172

if six years hadn't passed. Janet was there and, after the shock she'd had in the park, Kate did need someone to talk to.

Her smile had faded. She shrugged lightly. "To tell the truth, when I came back to Charlotte, I guess I did hope things would work out for Nathan and me." She bit her lower lip. "But now I know they aren't going to."

"Oh, that's such a shame! I never really understood what went wrong between you two. You really seemed to love him and he acted crazy about you."

Kate sighed. "Well, if he was, I guess I killed any feelings he had when I ran away from him."

"Why *did* you leave like that, Katie? I've always wondered. I mean, it just didn't make sense to me."

"I just couldn't cope with the guilty feelings I had after Phillip died. Until recently, in fact, I suspected he had killed himself deliberately because I'd broken our engagement. Sometimes I still wonder about it."

Janet gasped, reaching out to grasp Kate's right arm tightly. "Oh, no, Katie, I'm sure Phillip didn't kill himself! I never realized you thought he might have. And that's the reason you left Nathan? Oh, this is horrible. Oh, I wish I'd told you that . . ."

"Told me what?" Kate questioned when Janet's words abruptly halted. "What do you wish you'd told me? And how can you be so certain Phillip didn't kill himself?"

Janet shifted her feet uncomfortably then took a deep steadying breath. She released Kate's arm and smiled wanly. "All right, but first of all I want to say that I know Phillip was very fond of you. He just wasn't a very serious young man, even after the two of you became engaged. I guess I should have told you about the times . . . he asked me to go out with him, but I didn't know how to. Now, I wish I'd tried harder to find a way to tell you the truth."

Kate could scarcely breathe. "Are you saying Phillip tried to date you when he was engaged to me?"

"But I never went out with him, Katie! Honest, I wouldn't have done that to you. But . . . I did know other girls who dated him."

Kate could only stare at her friend. Two conflicting emotions pulled viciously at her. One was tremendous relief. Now she knew Nathan had been right about Phillip seeing other girls and that could only mean, with almost virtual certainty, that he wouldn't have committed suicide because of her. The last of her fears that he might have were erased, yet she still had to face the fact that by running away six years ago she had ruined any chance she and Nathan might have had to make their relationship permanent. And now it was too late to try to make amends. He was involved with Lydia again. What a stupid mess she had made of everything! Mentally berating herself, she chewed her nails but roused from her reverie when she noticed Janet was watching her with great concern.

"I don't know what to say," Kate murmured, "except that I'm glad you told me about Phillip. Don't they say it's always better to know the truth?" Glancing across the store, she caught a glimpse of Sue Latham and sighed regretfully. "I have to get back to work right now, Janet, but I do want to see you again soon. Do you think we could have lunch together one day this week?"

"Bill and I are going out of town tomorrow. We'll be gone through the weekend. But what about one day next . . ." Janet broke off with a startled gasp as Kate was suddenly, and with some violence, whirled around on the spot where she stood.

Kate's own surprised gasp caught in her throat and felt lodged there when she found herself staring up at Nathan's dark visage. The expression on his finely carved face could be described only as thunderous, and there was a storminess in his eyes rather frightening to behold. Kate's heart did a crazy little somersault, but she managed to produce a frown. "What the . . ."

"You're coming with me, Katie, and we're going to have a

nice long talk," he said chillingly after recognizing Janet with a brief nod. "Janet will excuse you, I'm sure."

"But . . ."

"Just walk, Katie," he commanded, a large hand gripping her upper right arm so tightly that she had no choice except do what he said.

As Katie was being whisked across the store, she looked back over her shoulder and saw Janet's startled expression altering to one of speculation.

"I'd appreciate it if you'd let go of my arm," Kate whispered heatedly, turning her head back to glare up at Nathan. "If you're so hell-bent on talking to me, I'd rather walk to your office instead of having you half drag me." When he didn't bother to answer or release her, then bypassed the bank of elevators and headed instead toward the exit that opened onto the back parking lot, Kate tried to dig her heels into the carpet. "Where do you think you're taking me?"

His answer was to jerk her forward and impel her out the exit into the bright afternoon sunshine and across the hot asphalt to his Jaguar. He opened the passenger door and the pressure of his hand at the small of her back issued its own unmistakable command. Deciding not to resist, Kate subsided into the bucket seat with an agitated sigh and crossed her arms over her chest when Nathan slipped in behind the steering wheel. She was determined to say nothing until he did and that resulted in a silence that grew ever more ominous and tense with each mile that they traveled. Still, Kate was too stubborn to speak even when they arrived at the house deep in the woods. She simply got out of the car and marched to the front door, leaving him to follow.

After Nathan unlocked the door, Kate went immediately into the den, stopped dead in the center of the room and turned around to face him. "Will this take long? I'm very busy. I have to see Sue Latham about . . ."

"Forget about Sue," he practically barked. "This is far more important than whatever business you have with her."

"Exactly what is *this* that's so important?" Kate inquired coldly. "I'd appreciate it if you'd tell me what it's all about."

"Suppose you tell me."

That cryptic response infuriated Kate. She longed to flail at him because of what she had seen in the park earlier, but she concealed that urge to commit violence and gave him a supremely haughty look instead. "I have no idea what you're talking about."

"I think you do."

"I do not, unless—unless you happened to overhear my conversation with Janet and know that she told me Phillip did date other girls while we were engaged and even asked her out several times. But why bring me out here just because I know the truth about that now?"

Now Nathan looked surprised and confused. Two long strides diminished the distance between them and he towered over Kate, his narrowed gaze searching her face. "Since you know that about Phillip, you surely can't still be wallowing in guilt. Does that mean you're not considering transfering back to Raleigh now?"

Now Kate believed she understood. "It's obvious Gary talked to you, but he neglected to mention that I never *seriously* considered a transfer."

"Why consider it at all?" Nathan raked his fingers through his hair. "It makes no sense, Katie. Last night you were going to move in with me, and today you were considering a transfer out of Charlotte."

"I was not going to move in with you. I said we'd talk about it," Kate corrected him icily. "By this morning, I'd already decided I wouldn't come here."

With his explicit curse, Nathan's eyes went a steely gray. "Tell me why, Katie."

"You tell me why you asked me to come stay in the first place."

"For heaven's sake, the reason should be perfectly obvious!"

"The only thing that's obvious to me is that you want me at your beck and call, available as a bedmate anytime you want me," Kate muttered accusingly. "Isn't that what you want, Nathan?"

His eyes never left her. "I guess you could put it that way."

Kate began to tremble with an anger that surpassed even the pain caused by his cruel admission. "What kind of fool do you think I am?" she exclaimed furiously, patches of scarlet color appearing on her cheeks. "You really think I'd let you use me that way? Oh, God, maybe I'd better go back to Raleigh. It would be the best thing for me to do, and I'm sure Lydia Plemmons would be overjoyed to see me leave Charlotte."

"I'm sure she would be," he conceded with a casual shrug of his shoulders. "But I'm afraid she's going to be disappointed in that respect. You are not returning to Raleigh. I'll never allow that."

"Never allow it?" Kate responded raspingly, clenching her hands into tight fists at her sides. "You don't own me! You're only my employer because you happened to buy the store where I was working. But just because you accidentally ran into me again after six years doesn't mean you can take over my life."

Nathan smiled humorlessly. "Accidentally, Katie? Do you really believe I was surprised to find you working at Renaldo's? Oh, no, I knew you were there; I never lost track of you once in the past six years. And when I acquired the Barron chain, I did it with the least amount of publicity possible, so you'd think Barron was acquiring Renaldo's. I didn't want you to know I had anything to do with it, figuring you'd probably quit Renaldo's and run away again. That was the last thing in the world I wanted to happen. I planned every step of it very carefully. Ours was no accidental reunion, Katie."

"*You planned all this?*" she exclaimed softly, her voice breaking, her face going pale with the sudden new fear that arose in her. "My God, did I injure your male ego so badly six years ago that you devised this intricate plot just to get revenge? Did you plan for us to become intimately involved again just so you could be the one to walk away this time?"

"Katie, listen," he began, starting to touch her face and sighing as she recoiled. "You don't understand . . ."

"Oh, Nathan, I knew you could be ruthless," she whispered, her tone anguished. "But I never imagined you could be as hardhearted and vindictive as this."

"Will you shut up and listen?" he growled, pressing fingertips against her lips as his free arm encircled her waist to draw her forcibly against him. "Maybe the desire for revenge had something to do with all the intricate plans I made, but as soon as I saw you again, I knew all I'd ever really wanted for six years was to have you back in my life again. Katie, I need you. I never stopped needing you. Oh, I tried, even became engaged to Lydia again, but once I realized she could never mean as much to me as you did, I called off the wedding."

"You called it off! Don't you mean she did? Because she couldn't forgive you for what you and I had done to her and Phillip, she married someone else and obviously lived to regret it. Now she's got you back, but you're standing there trying to con me into believing that you *need* me, have always needed me. You really must think I'm the most gullible idiot who ever lived. Now if you've had enough fun at my expense, I'll . . ."

"Be still, dammit, Katie," he ordered harshly, pinning her in his arms when she tried to jerk away from him. "What the hell do you mean about Lydia having me back again? For your information, she doesn't want me that way anymore than I want her. We're just friends."

"Hah! If you're just friends, why did she stare holes through me that night she came here? If looks could kill, I'd be dead and buried after the way she looked at me. Why all that animosity? If the two of you are no more than friends, then why should she dislike me so intensely?"

"You can hardly expect her to adore you, Katie," he murmured, beginning to move his hands over her back as she held herself stiff as a board against him. "After all, you're the reason I broke my engagement to her. Twice. Those were two humiliating experiences that didn't exactly make her love you. Or me either, for that matter. For years, she wouldn't even speak to me. It's only recently that we've become friends again."

"*Friends!*" Kate cried, hurt and exasperation intermingling. "Do you really expect me to believe the two of you are merely *friends*? After what I saw in the park today, I . . ."

"Ah ha, now I'm beginning to understand this little mix-up," Nathan said softly when Kate hastily snapped her mouth shut before finishing what she'd started to say. A smile played over his hard lips and he led her to a sofa, forcing her to sit down with him. Even as she struggled for freedom, he gently stroked her hair, looking deeply into her eyes as if he meant to will her to believe him. "You saw Lydia with me in the park today? You saw us kissing?" When she nodded and anger made her nostrils flare because he wouldn't release her, his smile deepened, etching attractive creases into his cheeks beside his mouth. "There is a reasonable explanation for that kiss, Katie."

"I'll just bet!" she retorted disbelievingly. "But why don't you try telling the lie so I'll know how laughable it is."

"You can be the most difficult young woman, love," he murmured, infuriating amusement edging his deep voice. "But my explanation isn't laughable because it happens to be the truth. Lydia asked to meet me in the park today because her ex-husband asked for a reconciliation. She wanted my advice, and when I told her precisely what she hoped I would—that a reconciliation certainly was worth trying—she kissed me. And that's all there was to it."

"Except that I don't believe a word you said," Kate said dully, wishing with all her heart that she could believe. She stared down at the buttons of his vest instead of meeting his gaze directly. "Since you bought Renaldo's, you've been playing cat-and-mouse games with me and obviously with Lydia too. Well, I'm going to do her a favor and stop playing. She won't have to despise me anymore because she'll have you to herself."

Nathan's expression darkened. "I've told you there's nothing between Lydia and me except friendship," he reiterated grimly. "But maybe you aren't willing to accept that as the truth, so you'll have an excuse to continue with your obsession about Phillip."

"As you once said, Phillip is in the past. And after what Janet told me today, I can leave him there. I know if he went out with other girls while we were engaged that he would never have even thought of crashing his car deliberately because of me. I'm still sorry I was very indirectly responsible for his accident because I had upset him, but I know I've done enough penance for that in the six years I lived with the horrible thought that he might have committed suicide." Meeting Nathan's piercing gaze, Kate shook her head emphatically. "Phillip's no longer my problem. Lydia is and the way you've been treating both of us for the past few weeks. You've used me and betrayed her, and now my problem is finding a way to cope with that fact."

"Then you have no problem," Nathan said soothing, cupping her jaw and rubbing the edge of his thumb across her soft lips, smiling as they involuntarily parted. "I haven't betrayed Lydia and I haven't used you. I love you, Katie."

As he lowered his dark head and lightly kissed her, Kate's traitorous body ached to respond, but with determination she pressed her lips firmly together again and drew back to look at him, eyes wide and reproachful. "I'm sure you tell Lydia you love her too. Maybe with her, you mean it," she said quietly despite the strangling tightness in her throat. "I know you see her often. Evelyn Hughes told me that, so no more games, Nathan, please."

"To hell with Evelyn Hughes," Nathan cursed softly, lean

fingers tangling almost roughly in Kate's silken hair. "She would have told you anything she thought would hurt you. She doesn't just exaggerate; she lies, Katie, and you, better than anyone, should know that. And if this feels like I'm only playing games with you . . ."

Kate's breath caught as, in a split second, Nathan wound her hair round his hand, tugged her head back, and took possession of her mouth, his lips parting her own with swift single-minded demand. Muscular arms imprisoned her, arching her slender supple body against the dangerous hardness of his as he scattered kisses over her face, down her neck, and whispered words of love between each of them. At last he lifted his head to gaze down at her, his breathing shallow and quick. "Now, Katie, tell me, did that feel like I was playing a game?"

"Passion isn't love," she whispered reprovingly. "You can say the words forever but unless you mean them . . ."

"How can I convince you I *do* mean them? Why can't you trust me and believe me when I tell you I loved you six years ago and I love you now?"

"If you loved me then, why didn't you come after me when I left?" Kate asked, voicing the question she had longed to ask for years. "You couldn't have loved me much if it wasn't worth your trouble to try to get me back. I wanted you to come find me. I hoped for that. If you had . . ."

"If I had, you still wouldn't have listened to reason about Phillip's death," he said impatiently. "Maybe now you think I could have changed your mind then, Katie, but I wouldn't have been able to. You were too young and impressionable; Evelyn had done a fine job of convincing you that you'd killed Phillip. I knew that."

"But . . ."

"Forget about all that. I can't change what you believed then, but I intend to change what you believe now. You think I don't love you but I do. Good God, Katie, I bought Renaldo's in

181

Raleigh for only one reason—to bring you back into my life. And although you deserved your promotion, I would have promoted you even if you hadn't earned it because I had to have you here in Charlotte where I could see you every day. Then I did everything in my power to try to get you to move out here with me, and I mean everything, except threaten to fire you if you didn't or get down on my knees and beg. Those are about the only two things I didn't try." He ceased talking for a moment, searching her face as an oddly sheepish expression appeared on his. "I even have to confess to lying about that jewel thief. He was already in jail when you checked into the hotel, but I hoped that if I omitted that little fact, you might be scared enough to come stay with me. Can't you see that only a man desperately in love with a woman would resort to a trick like that?"

As Kate stared at him, an unbidden surge of joy caused her heart to skip several beats but with the burgeoning of hope came the fear to give into it. Hope can be cruel when raised to the heights and then, as suddenly, dashed again. That possibility was too devastating to contemplate. If Nathan was only carrying out his game to the bitter end . . . No, she couldn't chance that. She averted her gaze from his beloved face before she could give in to the temptation to recklessly take a chance.

"You still don't believe me, do you?" Nathan questioned, cupping her face in his hands, making her look at him again. His smile was gentle. "Maybe this will convince you. The first time you came here, when you saw the mirrored dressing room, you told me you'd longed for a room like that when you were a child because you'd dreamed of being a prima ballerina. I already knew that, Katie. You told me six years ago, but the other day you left out some details I've always remembered, like the gold ballet slippers and the white tutu with gold sparkle scattered over it that you wanted very badly as a child too."

Kate's mouth opened slightly. Her eyes widened. He was right. The golden slippers and the besparkled gossamer tutu were details of her childhood fantasy even she had forgotten. But Nathan hadn't and suddenly the hope she tried valiantly to suppress surged out of control, although she wasn't really sure what he was trying to say to her. She could only ask him, her voice a breathless whisper, "What exactly are you telling me, Nathan?"

"I'm telling you I built that dressing room, this whole house, with you in mind, hoping that someday you'd live here with me," he whispered back then grinned endearingly. "Good heavens, Katie, why else would a bachelor like me want a mirrored dressing room?"

Kate's light answering laughter snapped the tension between them but soon her lips trembled and tears spilled. Soft sobs punctuated joyous laughter as she propelled herself into Nathan's arms, burrowing her face into the strong brown column of his neck while his arms tightened with wondrous possessiveness around her. Finally, after too many years alone, she was where she belonged again. It was almost as if she could feel love emanating from him, permeating her skin, and warming the very marrow of her bones and the most secret recesses of her spirit. Adoring him, she urged his mouth to hers once more and when the old familiar passion—the swift searing passion she now knew was born of love—flared between them, her caressing hands became as urgent and possessive as his.

Nathan cradled her in his arms across strong thighs, firm lips lingering on the delicate curve of hers until she felt alive with clamoring desires and was clinging to him. When he slowly released her mouth, her eyes fluttered open and she smiled up at him. "I love you, Nathan," she whispered. "So very much that I need to be closer to you. Take me upstairs to the deck. We've never made love outside in the sunlight, and right now that's all I want to do."

"I hope you don't expect me to refuse that invitation," he muttered huskily, standing with her securely in his arms and striding toward the stairs. He smiled rather wickedly at her. "If you did expect a refusal, then you've misjudged me again because I just might keep you up on that deck or in my bed and not let you go for several days at least."

"Promise?" she murmured hopefully. "Sounds like a terrific several days to me."

"My own shameless little hussy," he teased then kissed her lightly while ascending the stairs. "We'd be wise to spend one of the next few days making an honest woman out of you. That is, if you want to become Mrs. Nathan Cordell? Will you marry me, Katie?"

"Yes. But it'll have to be tomorrow. I have other plans for today," she said softly, lips curving into a provocative smile even as he kissed her again.

Five minutes later, dappled sunlight danced over them as they lay together on the chaise lounge. Nathan's eyes were dark and heavy-lidded as he surveyed the opalescent shimmer of creamy bare skin then sought the emerald depths of her own.

"Katie, how I love you," he said roughly. "I've been with you like this in so many dreams these past years that I'm almost afraid this is only another one of them and that I'll wake up soon and find you aren't really here. Are you sure that you can be happy here with me?"

"From now on, I'll always be here. The past can't hurt us anymore, Nathan. I know you've been right—and no one, not even Evelyn, can take away our happiness. What we have is real. Touch me and find out how real *I* am and let me show you how much I love you too," she invited, tears of joy and an abiding tenderness for him sparkling like diamonds where they caught in her lashes. She brought one lean brown hand up between her soft, curved breasts, and when his fingers pressed into her warm resilient flesh, she began her own exploration of his taut bronze body.

Some time later, with his filling of her and her eagerly yielding possession of him, they merged together in a lasting physical and spiritual commitment, all doubt vanquished by love. They reached a peak of ecstasy more keenly satisfying and fulfilling than they had ever before known, love and passion inseparable, predestined. Now Kate knew that Nathan had been right. There was indeed a vital bond between them, a bond of mutual love that had endured six long years of separation and was now a priceless certainty in the life they would truly share.

LOOK FOR NEXT MONTH'S
CANDLELIGHT ECSTASY ROMANCES ®

When You Want A Little More Than Romance—

Try A Candlelight Ecstasy!

Seize The Dawn

by Vanessa Royall

For as long as she could remember, Elizabeth Rolfson knew that her destiny lay in America. She arrived in Chicago in 1885, the stunning heiress to a vast empire. As men of daring pressed westward, vying for the land, Elizabeth was swept into the savage struggle. Driven to learn the secret of her past, to find the one man who could still the restlessness of her heart, she would stand alone against the mighty to claim her proud birthright and grasp a dream of undying love.

A DELL BOOK   17788-X $3.50

THE SEEDS OF SINGING
by Kay McGrath

To the primitive tribes of New Guinea, the
seeds of singing are the essence of courage.
To Michael Stanford and Catherine Morgan,
two young explorers on a lost expedition,
they symbolize a passion that defies war,
separation, and time itself. In the unmapped
highlands beyond the jungle, in a world
untouched since the dawn of time, Michael
and Catherine discover a passion men and
women everywhere only dream about, a love
that will outlast everything.

A DELL BOOK   19120-3 $3.95

Desert Hostage

Diane Dunaway

Behind her is England and her first innocent encounter
with love. Before her is a mysterious land of forbidding
majesty. Kidnapped, swept across the deserts of
Araby, Juliette Barclay sees her past vanish in the
endless, shifting sands. Desperate and defiant, she
seeks escape only to find harrowing danger, to
discover her one hope in the arms of her captor, the
Shiek of El Abadan. Fearless and proud, he alone can
tame her. She alone can possess his soul. Between
them lies the secret that will bind her to him forever, a
woman possessed, a slave of love.

A DELL BOOK   11963-4   **$3.95**

Bestsellers

- ☐ **ELIZABETH TAYLOR:** The Last Star
  by Kitty Kelley..................................$3.95 (12410-7)

- ☐ **THE LEGACY** by Howard Fast...................$3.95 (14719-0)

- ☐ **LUCIANO'S LUCK** by Jack Higgins...........$3.50 (14321-7)

- ☐ **MAZES AND MONSTERS** by Rona Jaffe...$3.50 (15699-8)

- ☐ **TRIPLETS** by Joyce Rebeta-Burditt...........$3.95 (18943-8)

- ☐ **BABY** by Robert Lieberman.......................$3.50 (10432-7)

- ☐ **CIRCLES OF TIME** by Phillip Rock.............$3.50 (11320-2)

- ☐ **SWEET WILD WIND** by Joyce Verrette......$3.95 (17634-4)

- ☐ **BREAD UPON THE WATERS**
  by Irwin Shaw....................................$3.95 (10845-4)

- ☐ **STILL MISSING** by Beth Gutcheon............$3.50 (17864-9)

- ☐ **NOBLE HOUSE** by James Clavell..............$5.95 (16483-4)

- ☐ **THE BLUE AND THE GRAY**
  by John Leekley.................................$3.50 (10631-1)

A woman's place—the parlor, not the concert stage! But radiant Diana Ballantyne, pianist extraordinaire, had one year before she would bow to her father's wishes, return to England and marry. She had given her word, yet the moment she met the brilliant Maestro, Baron Lukas von Korda, her fate was sealed. He touched her soul with music, kissed her lips with fire, filled her with unnameable desire. One minute warm and passionate, the next aloof, he mystified her, tantalized her. She longed for artistic triumph, ached for surrender, her passions ignited by Vienna dreams.

A DELL BOOK   19530-6 $3.50

Vienna Dreams

by JANETTE RADCLIFFE
